DANE
(Elementals CT MC)

ALEXI FERREIRA

Copyright © 2021 Alexi Ferreira

All rights reserved.

ISBN: 9798591765583

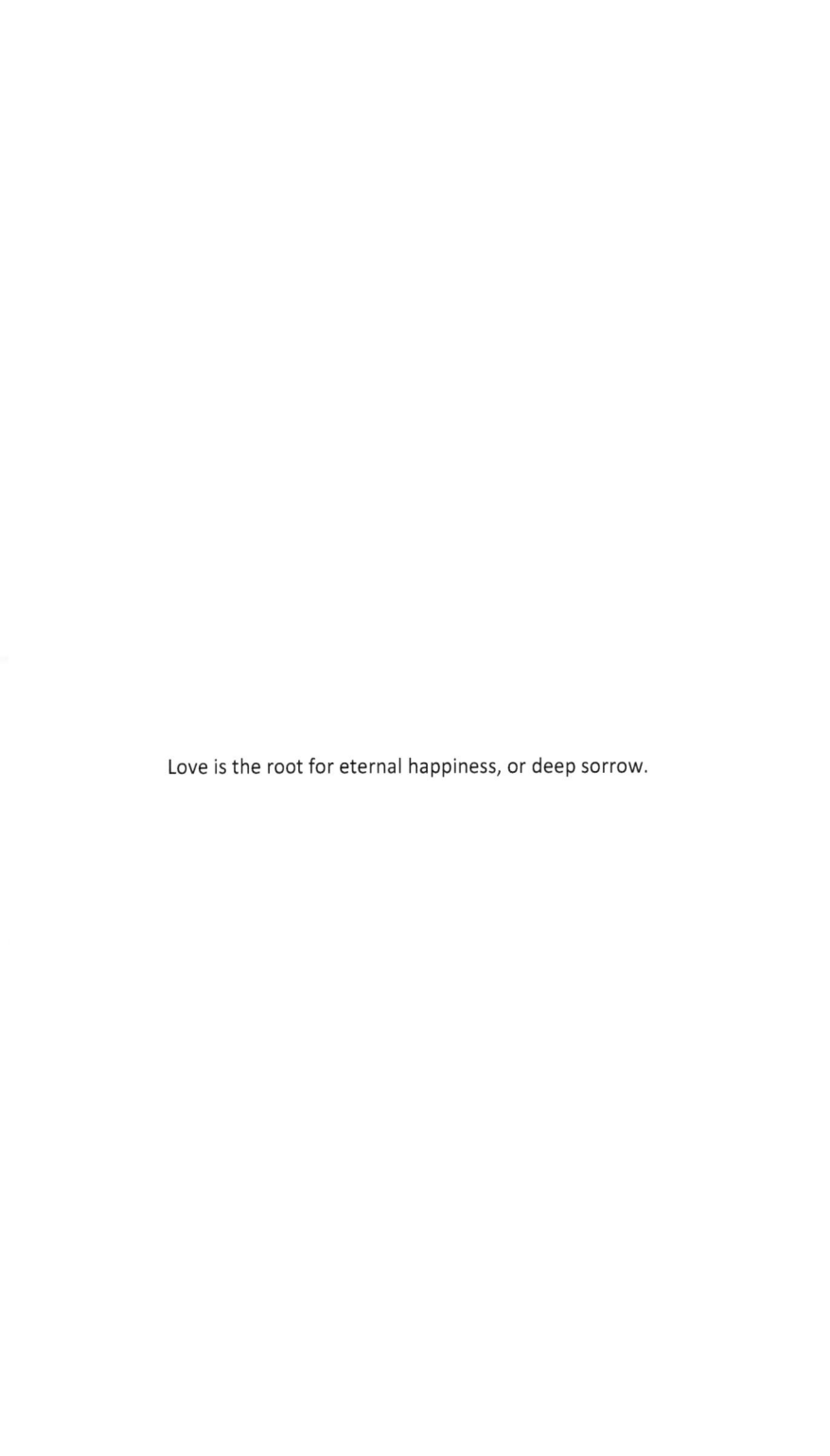

Love is the root for eternal happiness, or deep sorrow.

DANE 1	3
FREYA 2	15
DANE 3	27
FREYA 4	42
DANE 5	53
FREYA 6	65
DANE 7	76
FREYA 8	86
DANE 9	97
FREYA 10	108
DANE 11	120
FREYA 12	132
DANE 13	143
FREYA 14	156
DANE 15	167
FREYA 16	178
DANE 17	197
FREYA 18	208
DANE 19	223
A MESSAGE FROM ALEXI FERREIRA	232
DAG (Elementals CT MC) book 3	233
ESMERALDA 1	233

ACKNOWLEDGMENTS

Thank you to my kids that are my driving force. To all my readers for all their support, without all of you this dream wouldn't be possible, to my graphic designer JessFX for the great book covers and all your patience with me.

And a special thank you to A's Guardians, I am very blessed to have such wonderful ladies in my team, and to my wonderful PA's Sydnee Walsh and Mikki Thomas that keep me grounded and on schedule.

DANE 1

"Where the hell is this fucking woman?" Dag asks as we walk towards our bikes. Tor organized this security job to protect a fucking actress, but the woman seems to be oblivious to the fact that she might be in danger. To be honest, the last thing I feel like doing is babysitting.

"She's already a pain and we haven't even started," I mutter as I lean forward to start my bike.

This is good money for not much work. All we usually do is babysit whoever the next rich and famous is. There is hardly ever any violence and the only thing that might happen is a fan getting too excited and trying to hug the person we're protecting. Otherwise, these jobs are quite standard.

This one has been different from the moment it was

booked. From what Tor has said, the actress doesn't want any security, but her agent has insisted on it.

It looks like we might get a petulant, little, irritating female that thinks she's too good for everyone else and can order everyone around. Well, she can try, but she will fall short with any of us because one thing we don't do is take orders easily. As elemental's we are above the pettiness that humans usually have the habit of showing. Nothing irritates me more than a defiant human being. No matter if the truth comes up and slaps them in the face, they will purposefully be defiant for their own ego. Well, if this actress decides to be defiant, she will realize that she's dealing with the wrong men.

I twist the throttle of my Harley as we make our way towards where her agent is staying. If he wants us to protect her, he will have to tell us where to find the damn woman. After the constant search for the trafficking ring that is kidnapping women—women that could be possible mates to us Elementals; I was looking forward to having a break from it all, and just have an easy job where I can chill out and not have to think about all the women those fuckers have already been able to traffic.

We pull over at the Global Hotel. Apparently, the agent prefers to be served, but the actress wanted her own place to stay at while she was here in Cape Town. Luckily, the scenes she has to film will only need two weeks, as that was the time frame the agent gave us.

I'm extremely unprepared for this. I haven't even seen this actress's photo, but the others have all been briefed. I was lucky to have been assigned this job because Ulrich was the one who was supposed to be here, but now that he's bonded, staying away from his mate for long periods of time is out of the question.

"What's this fucker's name?" I ask as we make our way inside towards the reception desk.

"Mr. Taylor" Dag replies, stopping just in front of reception. It is clear by the receptionist's face that we are not the type of clientele they cater to at this hotel.

"Good Day, how may I help you?" The way the fucker is looking at us makes me want to punch his scraggly face. Placing my fists on top of the counter, I glare at him. He swallows, causing his Adam's apple to move nervously in his throat. His eyes shift between me and Dag, the realization hitting him that we're not wannabes, we're the goddamn real thing.

"Call Mr. Taylor down and tell him that the Elementals are here."

I see him tense at Dag's tone, but he reluctantly nods as he scrolls through his computer before dialling.

"Good Day, Mr. Taylor, we have two men in reception asking to see you. They say that they are the Elemental's." He suddenly turns, his voice lowering so we can't hear him. He doesn't realize that with us being elemental's, our hearing is way too sharp, therefore he could be hiding in a cupboard whispering and we would still hear him. "Are you sure, Sir?" he asks, glancing over his shoulder at us. "They don't exactly look like the type of people you would want to see."

Shaking my head, I stretch my arm out, my hand closing over the collar of the fucker that thinks he's better than us.

"Ohhh," he hisses in surprise as I snatch his collar and pull him off his feet. The asshole is so fragile that he loses his balance and falls back against the counter.

"Now, what is the room number?" I ask. He better not give me anymore dirty looks, or the asshole is going down.

"Two… two hun… hun… dred four."

I flick my wrist, which has him sliding down behind the counter in fear.

"Thanks," Dag says as we turn, making our way towards the lift. "Stuck up fucker," he mutters as we enter the lift.

"This chick is more of a problem than we expected," I growl.

I just want to chill with no complications for the next two weeks. She better not mess up that plan because I need a holiday. Stepping out of the lift, we make our way down the corridor until we find the agent's room. His door is ajar, which has me shaking my head at the idiot. We are in Cape Town, a country rift with crime, and the idiot leaves his room wide open for anyone to come in and help themselves to his stuff. It doesn't matter that this is a five-star hotel, he will be robbed blind here.

Walking inside, we stop when we find Mr. Taylor sitting on a recliner on his balcony. "Come on in, boys."

I tense, throwing Dag a frustrated glare. Do I look like a fucking boy? I'm three hundred and twenty fucking years old, and this asshole is calling me a boy? All because I'm a biker, and he thinks he's above us.

"Take a chill pill," Dag mutters, knowing that I would like nothing more than to show this asshole that he shouldn't be so trustworthy. Taking a deep breath, I grunt in reply as I come to a stop at the sliding door leading out to the balcony. Dag takes the other seat next to Mr. Taylor.

"We went to the location that was given to us, but your actress wasn't there."

He nods, a frown forms on his round face. "Oh, that useless PA of mine must have forgotten to inform you that Freya has moved." He picks up his phone from the table next to him and dials someone, putting it on speaker. "Julia, did you forget to inform the Elemental's of Freya's move?"

"I'm sorry, Sir, but I've just got back and..." the woman starts saying when she's interrupted by this pompous motherfucker.

"You're a useless piece..."

Dag pulls the phone out of the agent's hand, disconnecting the call.

"What are you..."

"Look, we want to start with this assignment, and you are wasting our time," Dag states. "Now, give us her address and we will be on our way, then you can go back to berating your PA."

I can see the man isn't used to being talked to like that, but he isn't stupid. He won't try his highhandedness with us again.

He stretches out his hand for his phone. "I need my phone. The address is on there."

Dag places the phone back in his hand, allowing him to find the address. "Thirty-two Augustus Road," he states.

"Why did you move her there?" I ask, curious to know if there was a threat involved and why she was moved to that area. I know Augustus Road, and I wouldn't exactly call that area upper class.

"Me? Move her? No, it wasn't me. She's an ungrateful bitch. Told me that she was moving because the house I got her was pretentious and she didn't need a five-bedroom house when it was only her living there." He shakes his head. "Can you believe that?"

Looks like this actress won't be as bad as I thought. Maybe we can have a relaxed time while we guard her. I hear footsteps outside and know that we have company. "Security is approaching," I grunt.

Dag nods, quickly standing up from the chair. "I would say that it has been a pleasure, but I would be lying," Dag says, following me towards the entrance of the room.

I hear Mr. Taylor murmur something in anger, but he doesn't stand up.

"There are two," I whisper, more to myself than to Dag as he can sense them as well as I can. I'm an air bender, therefore the variation in the air has me sensing its movement when someone disturbs it. Dag's an earth bender. He feels the vibrations on the ground which would have alerted him to the approach of the two security guards, too.

Stepping into the corridor, I turn to face the two men approaching. "Stop right there," they say. I could easily disarm them in the blink of an eye, but it would create more trouble than necessary. I shouldn't have knocked the receptionist down, but it was too tempting to resist. Tor is going to have a fit, but the look on the receptionist's face was worth it.

"Relax, the guy is fine we just had a meeting," Dag says, inclining his head towards the room.

"Mr. Taylor? Mr. Taylor, are you okay?" one of them calls out.

I hear the agent approach the door. "Gentlemen, what is going on?"

"Sir, these men accosted our receptionist, are you hurt?"

The agent shakes his head, coming to a stand before us in his flowing robe—such a pompous, slimy man. I hate working for people like him. If Tor didn't promise to rip out our balls if we messed up this arrangement, I would tell this asshole to keep his money.

"Put those guns down, they were just here for a meeting. I will make sure to compensate your receptionist."

The men look at each other, then one of them nods while pointing at us. "But, Sir, please understand, we ask you to please refrain from inviting these gentlemen here again."

Mr. Taylor raises his hand in peace. "They were just leaving." He looks over his shoulder at us. "Weren't you?" he says, gesturing his head towards the exit. The asshole thinks he is saving us.

I feel like punching through his pompous face. Walking

past him, I make sure to bump one of the security guards on my way out. I see him tense, but he thinks twice before attacking me. I'm not a small man, if anything, Tor and I are the tallest among our men. People are usually reluctant to approach us. As bikers, people automatically expect unruliness, which in our case they will get.

Walking out of the hotel, I see Eirik leaning against his bike in an outwardly relaxed stance. "You took your time," he mutters when we approach.

"Missed us?"

"The Desperados have been snooping around here," Eirik states as I sit on my bike. "Looks like they're after someone, too." The fucking Cape Town gangs are always up to no good, and no matter how much we try to stop them, it just seems like they grow an extra leg and branch out somewhere else.

"Well, we know where the actress is. Let's leave the Desperados to someone else," I grumble.

I'm on edge today. All I want to do is get to this actress, make sure she's protected, and relax. I'm fucking tired of fighting. Tired of the constant knowledge that evil is out there—evil that is always searching for another victim. No matter how much we fight, there is always more evil to find. That's why I need to find my mate. She's the only one that can bring me peace. There have been too many long years of loneliness in my past. No matter how many women I sleep with or how many parties I attend, I find no excitement in them anymore. I'm just exhausted.

When Ulrich found Anastasia, I must confess that I was jealous. At first, I felt sorry for him when I saw him fighting the bond between them, but then when I saw their connection grow, I felt a gap in my life—a gap that only a mate can close. Shaking my head, I grunt, picking my helmet up from the handlebars to slip it on.

Dag starts his bike then sits back as he slips on his helmet. When mine is on, I lean forward and start my bike. The familiar roar of the motor is pleasing to my ear, the drum of the motor vibrating through my body.

Dag pulls off first, and Eirik and I follow. The ride to the actress' house is short, therefore, we were there in no time. We pull up outside a typical Cape Townian, one storey house. The outside walls are bright orange, with a white strip across the top, everything about this place screams that she is trying to integrate into the community as a native, but there is nothing normal about this woman, if the comments I heard from the others are anything to go by. Climbing off the bike I grunt as I look around, but the neighbourhood seems pretty standard. What is she trying to do, hide among the middle class as one of them?

I feel a bolt of static rush through my body as I approach the door. What the hell is wrong with me today? I swear

I need a holiday away from everyone. As soon as this assignment is over, I'm telling Tor that I'm taking time out.

"There is someone at the back," Dag says as he turns to head around the house.

"Something is feeling off," I mutter. All my senses are in an uproar; I can't tell if it's danger as I feel them all over the place. Maybe I should get myself checked, because one minute I want to kill someone and the next I want to hug them. *What the fuck?*

"I don't sense anything?" Eirik says as he looks around before glancing my way. "Except your energy. What the fuck is wrong?" he asks just as we come around the house. I freeze when I see a slip of a woman, her back is to us and she's bending down to pull out a weed from the ground. Her jeans moulding that perfect ass, have my dick erect and wanting to burst through the zipper of my low-cut jeans. Her long auburn tresses obscure my vision of her face, but the tight cropped T-shirt she's wearing does nothing to hide her bountiful chest.

Something about her seems familiar—way too familiar.

"Hello," Dag greets as he stops a couple steps away from her. His voice has her jumping in surprise, gasping as she snaps around. Everything around me stills when I see her. Her mismatched eyes, one brown and the other blue, look at us in fear. "Don't be scared, sweetheart, we are your security. Mr. Taylor sent us." I feel a pull towards her that I've never felt before, it's like the tide pulling me in.

"Oh yes, he told me. I'm Freya, it's a pleasure meeting you." Her soft melodious voice feels like silk over my skin, every fibre in my body is now at attention. She takes a step towards us, tripping over the small spade that is laying on the ground from her gardening. Before she can fall, I rush towards her, my hands fitting around her waist to pick her up against me before she hurts herself. Her beautiful face turns towards me in surprise, and then her lips lift in a radiant smile.

"You're like me," she whispers. Her hand lifts, touching my cheek with the gentlest touch that I've ever felt. Suddenly, everything that I've been fighting for centuries, the tiredness, the anger, the very darkness that is my life, lifts away and in its place, I'm filled with a light of peace—a peace that can only be mine if given by my mate.

FREYA 2

The minute I touch him it feels like everything around me stills, but I know it hasn't because I hear the other man talking. His voice is faint and garbled because my focus is only on the man standing before me. He is a giant of a man, easily double my size. The smell of his leather kutte fills my lungs with an unmistakable fragrance of leather and sandalwood. His eyes capture and hold my attention, ever since I was a little girl, I've dreamt of his eyes.

I always thought that it was just a dream—a dream of a silly girl that just wanted someone to be the same as her and not labelled a freak. While at school, most people used to tease me about my eyes, and that is why I always wear contact lenses unless I'm alone like I thought I was out here. The paparazzi would have a field day if they found out about me.

I've worn coloured contact lenses for as long as I can remember—not even my agent knows that my eyes are different colours. But here is this man, he seems bigger than life and dares anyone to say anything about him being different. I wish I was like that; I wish I was courageous like him and could show the world that I'm different. Somehow, deep down, I knew he was out there somewhere because he and I were always destined to meet.

His skin under my hand feels so warm—so inviting. The feel of his stubble makes my fingers tingle in reaction. I want to stroke my fingers over the long, dark blond tresses that lie around his shoulders. On any other man, this long of hair might have looked feminine, but not on him. He is too male to ever look anything but rugged. There is a magnetism about him that is pulling me in— talking to something deep within me. I said to him that he was like me, and I've a feeling that he is more like me than I thought.

His fingers tighten gently around my waist as what sounds like a growl escapes him. His eyes are staring deep into mine and I feel like he is seeing right into my soul. "Are you okay?" His voice is deep, with a growly texture to it that seems to caress me.

Am I okay? I don't know. My mind seems to be focused only on this man, and even though I try to concentrate, I seem to be drawn to his energy alone.

"Who are you?" I ask, but I feel like my very soul already knows him. *How is that possible?*

"Dane," he replies, inclining his head against my palm. Only now do I realize that I'm still cupping his face, but I don't want to pull away. I don't want to break the connection I'm feeling with this man. It feels right—it feels like home.

"Can you feel it?" I whisper, worried that he is going to think I'm a fruit cake, but I need to know if I'm the only one feeling our connection. One of his eyebrows arches, followed by a curt nod. My head spins as my vision goes blurry, but instead of being worried of my sudden decrease in focus, I know that everything will be okay. My body shakes as if I'm ill with a high fever and my legs give way, but Dane is there to catch me, cradling me up against his chest.

My head falls against him.

"What the fuck is wrong with her?" I suddenly hear the world around me once again as my body convulses.

The rumbled words vibrating through Dane's chest penetrate my very soul. "She's mine."

"Fuck," someone says, but it sounds like it's coming from a long distance away. I'm not sure if I lose consciousness, but the next thing I know, something warm is trickling into my mouth and down my throat. I still feel the warmth of Dane's arms around me, so I ignore the fear of whatever has me reacting like this and trust that whatever it is, is meant to be.

"Everything is going to be okay," I hear Dane say close to my ear. "I'm right here." The assurance that he isn't going anywhere has me succumbing to the darkness, knowing that Dane will be here to look after me until I'm feeling like myself again.

***

I don't know how long I've been out, but the first thing I feel is heat radiating all around me. I know that I'm still in Dane's arms, even though I haven't opened my eyes. I don't know what happened earlier, but I swear I must be going mad because I'm sure that I can feel a connection with this man. Opening my eyes, I see him looking down at me. His hair falls over his face, placing it in shadows. Even with his hair concealing his features, I can still see his intense eyes boring into me.

"How are you feeling?" I didn't dream the reaction his voice has on my senses, it's like a live wire sharpening every cell inside my body.

"Fine, but what's going on?" I see him frown; I get the feeling that he is contemplating on what to tell me.

"This is going to sound strange to you, but you were made for me, you are my woman."

Maybe with anyone else it might sound strange, but not with me. I've been living a strange life ever since I was a teenager, and there isn't much I find strange anymore. When I was twelve, I realized that I could do something no one else could. I tried to tell my mom, but she put it down to having a very fertile imagination until one day I could show her. After that, I wished I hadn't because from then on, our relationship changed.

My mom and I don't speak much now. She doesn't say it, but I know she thinks I'm a freak. I also know that she loves me, but fears what I can do. Will this man think I'm a freak and leave? Maybe I should just not tell him anything, it's not as if he'll ever find out unless I tell him.

How do you tell someone that you're able to freeze everything around you—even him? How would that make him feel? I don't think anyone would want to be near someone that can do that. I found out that I could make everything around me come to a standstill when I was twelve. I was upset because a girl, that I thought was my friend, posted a picture of me, and on the photo it stated *beware of the witch*.

I was already weary of those around me, but that changed me. I don't trust people easily, and I sure don't get close to anyone anymore. So, this feeling that I'm having with Dane is completely new to me—a feeling of oneness I can't exactly explain. Not even with my own mother do I feel that. "It doesn't sound strange. I feel something with you that I've never felt before. How is that possible?"

"I'm an Elemental. We Elemental's mate for life." His words are firm, as if to ascertain their truth.

"What does that mean?"

"It means that I'm not completely human. I'm stronger, faster, and can bend air to my will."

I tense at his words. Is it possible that he is as different as I am? Is this someone playing a prank on me or did someone find out what I can do and is trying to test me?

"Show me." If he really is as he says, then it won't be a problem for him to demonstrate it.

He suddenly raises his hand, motioning for me to look behind me. Glancing over my shoulder, I only now realize that we are inside the house, and that the other men that were with him are nowhere to be seen. We are on the two-seater couch—Dane's girth taking up most of it. I'm about to turn back to Dane when I see the door opening. It moves the other way again as if someone was closing it, and just when I thought it would stop, he opens it again.

"Are you doing that?"

"Yes."

"Do something else." I need to make sure that it is him moving the door.

The door stops moving and then one of the couch pillows that must have been thrown on the floor when Dane came to sit here, lifts into the air, moving towards us. My mouth hangs open as the pillow drops onto my lap. Looking up at Dane, I can feel myself smiling. Finally, there is someone like me in this world! I throw my arms around his neck, hugging him tightly. He probably finds my reaction strange, but he has no idea how relieved I am to find someone different like me.

"If I get this reaction from you with a little trick like that, then I will make sure to keep you entertained for the rest of our lives," he says, which has me leaning back and looking up at him just as his head lowers to kiss me. It's a kiss that overwhelms my every thought. I've never been kissed like that before. The only kisses I've experienced are while filming the movie I'm here for, and I swear I would rather be licking an ashtray than kissing my co-star Kane.

His hand cups the back of my head as he deepens the kiss. Dane is so much bigger than me that it feels like I'm engulfed in his arms. He makes me feel protected, dainty, and very feminine. I've had many men ask me out, and I've even gone out on a few dates, but I've never got close enough to go on a second date. There was always something that repelled me about them, but with Dane, I feel like I want more.

I can feel his hardness under my ass, and instead of retreating, I want more. I've never been with a man before—something that would have the paparazzi going crazy if they ever found out. I'm old-fashioned and never felt the need to sleep with anyone just because. I want my first time to be with someone that calls to me—someone that makes me lose my mind with passion and I think I've just met that someone because I'm not thinking much right now, just feeling.

Dane lifts his head; his eyes are heavy with passion while he looks through me. "You are mine. I know it sounds strange, and that it's going too quickly, but you will see with time that we are better together than apart." Why is it that his words resonate so true with me? I've never been one to trust or believe blindly on what is told to me, but with Dane, it seems like I'm aware of him on a deeper level than I know.

"But we don't even know each other."

"Our souls know each other. All the rest will follow." He is about to lower his head again when there is a loud crash, as if glass is breaking. I feel his body tensing below me. One minute I'm sitting on his lap, the next I'm on the ground and Dane is shielding my body. I can feel his muscles flexing as his head turns towards the windows.

"Dane," I hear a man call as the door bursts open and one of the men from earlier appears. "Are you guys okay?"

I hear a deep growl escape from Dane as his head snaps up to face the man. "What the fuck happened?" I can feel the anger vibrating through him as he continues to hover over me.

"Two motherfuckers in a van threw a brick through the window."

My body tenses. I've been threatened in the past, that's why I was assigned bodyguards, but I never thought it would amount to a real threat.

"Dag went after them, but I doubt he will be able to catch up as they were long gone when he took off."

Dane simply nods, which has the man turning and walking into the dining room where I'm guessing the brick is. Dane stands, and then he is helping me up to my feet. "Are you okay?" he asks, looking at me carefully, which has my stomach knotting in pleasure. I can sense the anger pulsing through him, but he still takes the time to see if I'm okay.

"Yes, thank you."

"The information we got was that you had been threatened, but nothing was reported that there had been more than just threats."

"That's because there hasn't been," I say as I lift my hands to push a strand of hair back from my face. "I mean, there have been threats but not any real evidence that it was more than just someone being mean."

"I'm going to kill that son of a bitch."

At Dane's threat, I tense. "Who?" I ask in surprise at his obvious anger.

"Your fucking agent. He didn't tell us you were actually being threatened."

That has me shrugging. I know that Tom isn't the nicest person. If I could go back, I would never have gotten involved with him, but he knows how to make money and how to promote his actors. Therefore, I've let him manage my career, and when these threats started arriving, I didn't pay any attention to them because we get strange mail all the time, but Tom thought it was best to get me some security. Never in a million years did I think that it would be Dane, or I would have asked for security myself.

I confess that at first, I was against it, but with Tom sometimes it's pointless arguing. "It was just a few notes, and someone scratched the car I'm driving," When I see how Dane's body stiffens, I try to disarm the moment. "To be fair, it could have been random."

"From now on, if anything happens, I want to know about it," he states as he takes a step towards me. Dane is a threatening presence, especially when he's as angry as he is now. I've only just met him, but I can tell that he would make lesser men shake with his presence alone, but even though I sense the danger that he can bring to others, I somehow feel safe in his presence.

"Most times, I don't know about these things as all my mail is sorted by a PA. The only reason I found out about the threats was because of the scratch on my car."

"I will have a talk with your agent," he states as he takes another step towards me. Looking up, I see his body is still tense with anger, but there is something else in his eyes. "Freya, I want you to know that no matter what I will protect you, but you need to listen to what I tell you."

I'm not someone that follows blindly, but Dane has me trusting him from the minute we met. If he tells me to listen to something he says because it will keep me safe, then I will consider it, and if it makes sense to me, I will definitely follow his guidance.

"Okay, Dane," I murmur as he lifts his hand to cup my cheek. The minute his fingertips feather over my skin; I feel a friction of electricity race down my body. The man's touch makes everything around me disappear. When I make people freeze, this precise thing happens, but then the person wouldn't be stroking my cheek or lowering his head to kiss me. Dane somehow triggers my powers, but not in any specific way that I can pick up on. He's a beacon of light in a world I thought covered me in darkness. It's the same feeling I get when I've stopped someone from doing something wrong, giving me a sense of purpose in this cruel, awful world. It's not cruel anymore. How can it be cruel when it gave me someone like Dane?

DANE 3

Fuck, my woman is beautiful. The minute I touch her, that hole I had in me seems to fill with light. I'm not a saint. I've lived my life fighting evil, but I also enjoy living my life to its fullest. Freya might not approve of some of the things I've done before, or some that I might still need to do. As Elementals we fight evil at every turn, but we also don't stick to normal human conventions. Freya might find the others difficult to understand because we can be coarse and violent at times, but as my woman, she will soon realize that my brothers will protect her with their lives because she is now part of me, or she will soon be.

I need to complete our bond, every cell in my body is fighting wanting Freya. Her fragrance surrounds me, her beauty bedazzles me, and her voice calms the constant fury that was my life. "I want you." I know that maybe I should take our mating slow—Freya doesn't even know me, but the way we are both drawn to each other, I'm sure that she wants me just as much as I want her.

I can see her cheeks darken with colour at my words. Being an actress, I can only imagine how many men must have already told her the same thing, but she will soon find out that I'm going to be the only man for her from now on. If another man even thinks about touching her, he will be dead.

"What about the other men?" Her eyes snap towards the door where Eirik appeared earlier. I tense, none of my brothers would ever think of interrupting us while I'm bonding with my woman. The only reason Eirik even appeared at the door earlier was because of what happened, but she wouldn't know that.

"Eirik won't come in here again."

"Umm, maybe we should go to my room." Her innocence is endearing, I can sense that Eirik is no longer in the house, therefore, he wouldn't be hearing any of our lovemaking. But if my woman wants to be in a more private setting, I will grant her wish because I want our first time together to be memorable for her. Lowering my head, I take her lips in a gentle kiss as I place my hands around her waist, picking her up off the couch. Turning, I make my way out of the sitting room and down the corridor where I'm guessing her room must be.

This house is different from the other one we went to first, but it's much more to my taste. I'm pleased that she isn't into the whole pretentious lifestyle most celebrities absorb themselves in. "Where?" I ask as I break the kiss. Her legs are tucked firmly around my waist while her womanhood rubs against me. I swear if we don't make it to the room soon, I will take her right here against the wall. I've never been so hard and horny like I am right now. Fuck, I know that finding your mate messes with your mind, body, and senses, but Freya is completely messing with my very world.

"Here," she murmurs as she glances at the door we are walking past. Turning, I shoulder the door open of the room and step inside. Freya hasn't been here long because the room is sparse, but I have better things to do right now than to look at the décor. Pulling the door closed with my foot, I take the couple of steps needed to lay Freya on the bed.

Her beautiful eyes are heavy with passion as they look up at me, hair spreading out on the pillow around her. Her gorgeous, swollen lips are the only evidence that she has been kissed thoroughly. I place my hands on her waistband, pulling her jeans down over her waist, calves, and finally onto the floor. Her tiny white panties encase her womanhood, showing me just enough to have me wanting to tear them off. But for some reason, I want to go slow with Freya and take my time. My fingers stroke up her smooth legs as I kiss her ankle, then slowly move up her calf until they're sliding underneath her shirt. My lips kiss her covered pussy. I hear her intake of breath when I kiss her again. My hands cover her breasts, tweaking her nipples under what feels like a lacy bra.

"Ohh," she exclaims as I take the hem of her tiny panties between my teeth and start pulling it down. Her fingers entwine in my hair. "Dane."

The slight pull of my hair has my self-control slipping. Lifting her ass up, I pull her panties the rest of the way down and off her beautiful body, then I am undressing faster than I've ever undressed before. When I turn, I freeze. Freya is sitting up on the bed, her breasts free of all coverings. Her eyes are roving over my body, and I'm sure the expression on her face is one of pleasure. My arms and back are covered in tattoos, but the rest of my body is free of ink. I've always thought of leaving my chest free to add my mate's name and any children that we might have together. Now that I've found Freya, her name will go over my heart. She is my woman, and I will make sure that everyone knows it.

"Damn, woman, you are beautiful," I whisper as I place my knee on the bed.

Her hand lifts to touch my biceps, eyes rising to look up at me. "And you are perfect in every way."

To know that my woman wants me, pleases me. I know that her being my mate has her unconsciously drawn to me, but finding your mate attractive is not part of it. Her hand on my stomach has warmth spreading throughout my body. My cock flexes, causing precum to drip out. It shines gloriously in the light that filters in through the window. I slip my hand around the back of her neck, leaning her head further back so I can take her lips in a blistering kiss that leaves us both hot. Her fingers move over my abs and down my chest while her other hand strokes the leg I have on the bed.

All my senses want her hand to move to where I need it most, but I've never been a patient man so breaking out of our kiss, I push her down on the bed, leaning over her so my lips can take her perfect nipple into my mouth while my palm moves over her stomach to her mound. A little triangle of auburn hair tickles my fingers as I slip them through the hair between her folds. Her legs are closed, but I can still feel the moistness that has pooled between her legs. Her little love bud is begging to be stroked.

Her hand moves to my head as I lick and nibble at her breast, enjoying her gasps of pleasure. Her hips rise gently as I stroke her pussy. My erection is painful, but I ignore it. I want to make this first time for my mate perfect. It will be the first time for the rest of our very long life together.

Her fingers slide down over my stomach to my cock. She tenderly touches me, then retreats the tease. I'll show her not to tease me, the minx. Slipping my finger into her heat, I hear her gasp and body tense. Fuck, she's so tight.

Her hand suddenly tightens around my cock, which nearly has me coming in it. Fuck me, I feel like a fucking teenager not able to control himself. Moving down between her legs, I slide between them; my fingers gliding over her smooth calves and up to her hips so I can raise her slightly before raking my cock over her wetness.

"Dane, ohh." She raises her torso. Her breasts elevate, catching my eye.

"Freya, look at me."

She opens her eyes that are heavy with passion. I slide into her heat, feeling her tightness grip me. She's like a… fuck no. I tense, stopping when I feel a barrier.

"Freya?" I must be mistaken, she can't be a virgin, can she? I'm about to pull back when she suddenly lifts her hips, the movement has me burying myself deep within her heated body.

"Dane," she rasps out. Shit. I don't think I can stop now that I'm finally one with her. Her hips move slowly once again.

"Don't move, sugar," I say, "let me just… shit, you moved." I can't stop. Now I really need to move. Sliding out slowly, I feel every single muscle of hers tighten around me. When I'm halfway out, I stop to check on her. "Are you okay?" I ask, sliding in again. Damn, her fucking body is perfect.

"That feels so good."

At her comment, I throw all caution to the wind. Pulling out slowly, I thrust forward, out, then in again. My movements quicken. This isn't going to take as long as I would like, but I can't hold back. Pulling my arm to my lips I tear at it with my teeth until there is a gash that starts to bleed, placing my arm over Freya's lips I see my blood drip onto her lips, which has me ready to burst as my balls tighten after seeing my woman devour my life force.

"Dane?" she gasps in question, but she's wound so tight, ready to explode in pleasure that she isn't thinking of what is happening.

"I join us forever and always. Where one goes, the other shall follow. I will hold you above everyone and everything else. I will protect you until my last breath. My body, soul, and mind are forever yours and yours is mine," I say those words that will bind our life force just as I feel Freya come undone under me. Her pussy spasms, tightening even more around my pulsing cock.

My control evaporates completely as I grunt, letting myself explode deep within her heat as I bite into her shoulder to take some of her blood and connect us forever.

I've never felt this feeling of fulfilment like I do in this very moment, or the protectiveness that I feel towards this woman that is now my mate—for always.

Freya's breathing is still erratic. Her eyes close as a sweet smile forms on her face. I can't believe I'm her first. The overwhelming possessiveness that fills me is all consuming. Us Elementals are naturally possessive but to know that my woman has only been with me, it's like gold to a leprechaun.

"You were a virgin." My statement has her tensing and her eyes opening.

"Yes."

"Thank you, I will treasure the memory."

Her cheeks are rosy with embarrassment, giving her that look of innocence that I now understand. "I had no idea it could be like that," she whispers, her hand now rising to cover her breasts. I take her fingers and interlace them with mine, noticing how my hand engulfs her much smaller one and how her petite, perfect body looks so tiny next to mine. The contrast pleases me, giving me a protective sense.

"It isn't, but we are mated, therefore, our joining will always be special."

She frowns at my statement. "Guess you would know," she says, biting her lip. "A man like you must have lots of women after you." I know that our women, once mated, can be as possessive of us as we are of them, that's why I would rather not get into my past with her because I haven't been a saint, but I know that from now on there will only be one woman for me.

"The past is just that, the past. You are my future and the only woman for me. Trust me when I say that as Elemental's we only bond once and it's for eternity." Any other woman's energy once we are bonded repulses us.

"Tell me more about yourself, I've just had sex with a man that I only met a couple of hours ago. Trust me when I say that I'm never like that." I lift my hand to stroke her cheek. She turns her face into my palm which pleases me at her complete acceptance of our bond. I know that with most of my brothers who have bonded before, their mates had difficulty accepting them and the whole mating concept, but Freya is taking it in stride.

"Why have you believed me so easily?" I have to ask because I've thought a lot over the years about how I would convince my mate to join me once I found her, and she found out about what we are. Never once did I think it would be this easy.

"Because I'm different too, and I always thought that I couldn't possibly be the only one. So, when you showed me you were different, it was a confirmation that I was right."

"How are you different?" I can see the hesitation in the way she tenses—the way she looks away. I don't think her being different has been easy for her, I will make sure that from today onwards, she understands that being different is a gift to us and nothing to be hidden.

"Hey, whatever it is, trust me when I tell you that we have some really amazing women in the Elemental's that have very special gifts of their own. Whatever your gift is will be accepted and appreciated by all of us."

Her eyebrows raise in surprise. "There are more?" She lets go of my hand and sits up. I can see the curiosity in her face.

"Yes, there are quite a few more."

I frown when she winces and places her hand over her arm. I thought she had sat up because she was curious, but it seems like there is another reason altogether. "Are you okay?"

She nods and then looks at her shoulder and upper arm as she rubs it. "Yes, must be some kind of insect bite." I look at her shoulder seeing a slight tinge of red appear only then do I remember the mark.

"Fuck, I forgot."

At my angry tone, her gaze snaps back to mine. "Forgot what?"

"The mark," I grunt as I slide her hand away, placing my much bigger one over the area that is already feeling hot to the touch. "When we find our mates and bond with them, our mark appears. See, this one is mine." I turn my shoulder slightly for her to see the unique mark that runs from my shoulder down my arm, the interlinked symbols a pattern of unimaginable beauty. All Elemental's have their own unique birthmark in that spot. When we bond for the first time, our women acquire that same birthmark for all to know who she belongs to.

"What exactly are you saying?" she asks, her voice strained. "It's burning! What the hell is happening?"

"You are getting a mark like mine."

She glares. "Are you kidding me? Is it going to look like that?" I look at my arm, surprised that she sounds so put out. I always thought my mark was beautifully intricate, never once did I think that my woman wouldn't like it.

"What's wrong with it?" There's a defensive note in my voice.

"I can't have tattoos, It's in my contract." She gasps in pain. "It's burning!" I hate knowing that she's in pain. A feeling of uselessness fills me—a completely new feeling for me, one I don't like.

"It will get better soon," I promise as I bend the air around her shoulder, willing it to rotate and cool her down. After what feels like an hour, but couldn't be more than a few minutes, she starts to relax. I can see the same intricate marks starting to become visible on her. It's the same as mine, only smaller.

"Please tell me it will go away," she pleads as she looks up at me from the mark on her arm.

"No… I thought you would like it." I was clearly wrong.

"Like it?"

Why is she looking so flabbergasted?

"You know what I do for a living, don't you? I can't have an arm with tattoos, no matter how lovely it is."

"Well, that's just too bad because now you do." I pull away from her to get up. I don't like the idea that she doesn't want my mark on her, and when I think about her profession, I don't like the idea of it either.

"Okay, maybe tell me what else to expect," she says, leaning down to pull the duvet up over her nakedness, which I also don't like. My mate shouldn't be hiding her body from me. Lifting my hands, I shove my fingers through my hair, feeling the slight pain when they encounter a knot.

"I'm part of the Elemental's Cape Town MC. By all form and intent, we are a normal MC, but as Elemental's, we can all bend specific elements." I see her frown at my revelation. "I'm three hundred and twenty years old." At this, she gasps, her eyes widening in surprise.

"Are you serious?" It still amazes me how she will just believe everything I say.

"Yes." I know that she's twenty-five from what I heard about her from Dag, but nothing prepared me for the innocent that she is. "We only mate once in our very long lives, and when we do, that is it for us. You, Freya, are my mate."

"What happens when I die, can't you mate again?" Her question makes me tense, my anger rising at the mere thought of anything happening to her.

"You will not die, and if anything were to happen to you, I would die with you. Our energy is now linked. You are the light to my darkness. Without you, I will not want to exist."

"But your life will now be so much shorter because you have mated with me."

I shake my head. "No, Freya, you have taken my blood and will continue taking it periodically. This will keep you living as long as I do. You will never die like humans do." She raises her hand to the spot where I bit into her shoulder to take some of her blood—a bruise is already forming.

"Are you a vampire?"

I grin. "No, we don't live off drinking blood, but our mates do need to take some of our blood sometimes just to keep them healthy. When you take our blood, you don't get sick like humans do, you don't age, and you feel stronger."

She raises her hand to her face, stroking a finger over her forehead. "Are you saying that I will look like this for as long as I live?"

"Yes, you look beautiful."

She frowns. "What else is there?"

"I won't accept any other man touching you. You are mine."

"Does that work both ways?" she asks with a raised brow

"Yes. From now on, you are the only woman for me. That is the truth." I know that she doesn't seem to believe that part, but with time she will see that it's the truth.

"You do know that as an actress we sometimes film

scenes with men... kissing scenes."

The thought of any man coming near her with his lips has my whole body rigid, ready to fight any asshole that thinks he can kiss her.

"There will be no more of that."

She gasps at my statement, her shoulders straightening. "Well, I'm afraid that there will be, because I've got a contract and the movie that I'm filming has a romantic encounter with someone."

Her words have me taking a threatening step towards the bed. "If anyone touches you, they will be dead." I want her to understand that I'm not joking about this, if I see any man touching her, I will make sure the fucker never breathes again.

"You can't do that," she whispers in an angry voice. "It's just work."

I bend so my face is closer to hers. "Dead," I state before straightening up and turning to pick up my clothes from off the ground.

"You didn't tell me that you were such a troglodyte," she snaps just as I grab my boots and walk out of the room buck naked, closing the door behind me. I'll get fucking dressed in the corridor, and what the fuck is a troglodyte?

FREYA 4

I've never felt as alive, as excited as I do right now. I know that I'm over my head in this—that Dane is more than I think I can handle, but he pulls me in like a moth to light. He makes me feel things that I never thought were possible to feel. Walking back to the bedroom after drying my hair, I look at myself in the mirror. Tom is not going to be happy when he sees the mark on my arm. I rub at my arm but nothing, how can this happen? How is it possible for a tattoo to appear out of nowhere? Rubbing again I shake my head. The mark doesn't rub off or wash off, there is no way of getting rid of Dane's mark.

Tomorrow, I have to go in, the scene is a sexy kissing one. How the hell am I going to wear a strapless top with my arm filled with tattoos like it is? And what am I going to do about Kane, would Dane really kill him? I don't think so, but he looked serious enough when he said it. I will just have to make sure that Dane isn't allowed where we will be filming tomorrow. Maybe one of the other men will guard me while we are there.

To be honest, I think Tom is going a little overboard with the whole security stunt, but I also didn't expect them to throw a rock through my window and they did. Security is tight when we are filming so I doubt I will have any trouble on set. Taking in a deep breath, I smile. I never thought I would be sleeping with someone when I woke up this morning or that I would be mated to a hunky troglodyte, but life has a strange way of changing our plans. I still need to tell Dane about my abilities, but we got side-tracked when I was going to tell him. After everything that happened with the tattoo on my arm. I think I'll be okay with thinking that he is used to different.

Looking at the door I sigh. Well, I guess I've hidden away long enough. I wonder if Dane will still be mad? Straightening my shoulders, I make my way out of the room and down the corridor towards the sitting room, only to come face-to-face with the other man that I had seen when they first came into the garden. I can feel my cheeks heating with embarrassment, wondering if he knows what Dane and I did.

"Umm, hi," I whisper shyly.

He grins. "Hey beautiful."

His words make me stiffen. Does he know I'm with Dane?

"Do you know where Dane is?"

"He's on a call, he will be in shortly," he states as he inclines his head towards the kitchen. "Why don't we go into the kitchen?" I nod.

As I make my way in there, I find the other man who came in to tell us about the brick, already in there.

"I'm sorry but I don't know your names," I tell them awkwardly, not remembering if they introduced themselves already or not. In my defence, when I saw Dane everything became blurry.

"I'm Dag, and this is Eirik"

Dag has the most amazing blue eyes, and with his black hair and tanned skin, the contrast is hot to say the least. When I look at Eirik, he is just as handsome, but in a deep tormented kind of way. I can see tattoos on his neck and both of his arms starting from where the sleeves of the T-shirt end. I'm certain that the rest of his body is just as tattooed. His short, dark brown hair suits his square jaw, and at first, I thought his eyes were blue, but now I'm thinking that they are more grey than blue.

"Are both of you like Dane?" I whisper, not sure if I should be asking this or not.

Dag leans near me as if to tell me a secret, then he points at his chest. "Earth." His hand turns, pointing at Eirik. "Water."

Oh, this is so exciting.

I jump in surprise at Dane's angry words coming from right behind us. "Get the fuck away from my woman."

Dag lifts his hands in the air with a smirk on his face. "I was just introducing myself and Eirik."

Dane grunts as he comes to stand next to me. Looking up at his face, I see a muscle ticking by his jaw. *Is he still angry at me?*

"Guess the call didn't go well?" Eirik asks

"Let's just say he's not in the best of moods," Dane grunts with a shrug. "We are to maintain our course unless absolutely necessary."

"Well then, guess we are here for a while," Dag murmurs as he walks towards the fridge and opens it. I hear him groan before he glances back. "We need to order food."

His statement has me frowning, the fridge is full of food. "You can use the food in there," I offer. If they are here to keep me safe, the least I can do is feed them.

"No offense, Beautiful, but the stuff in there isn't food."

I frown at his statement, there is a fridge full of fresh fruit, yoghurts, vegetables, and juices. What could he possibly want?

"Get ready, Brother, I think your woman is going to have you on a diet soon."

I gasp. "What makes you say that? There's a lot of healthy food in there."

"That's the problem… it's all healthy!" he says with a raised brow

"Just order the fucking food, Dag, stop quibbling," Dane grunts before slipping his arm around my shoulders, guiding me towards one of the chairs at the dining table.

"We need you to tell us what your movements are for the next week, so we can prepare," Eirik says as he sits down in front of us. I'm not someone that likes to party or has many friends, so my life is quite boring. If they think that they'll get to go out a lot because I'm an actress, they will be disappointed.

"I'm afraid that most of my time will be on set or here. I don't have any other commitments besides the two weeks before we finish filming this movie." Dane's fingers are now massaging my neck lightly which is distracting.

"Great, so all we need to do is accompany you to set, make sure that no one comes near you, and we are good," Eirik states

"Well, on set there will be people near me all the time, but that is normal as we work together." I need them to realize that I'm not going to stop my normal routine because of this threat.

"What exactly is your role in this movie?" Dag asks, sitting down next to Eirik.

"Well, the movie is a romantic comedy. It's a romantic entanglement between a group of friends, where one guy likes two women. I'm one of those women. We have filmed everything already, and we just need to get the final bits in before we are done."

"Give me action any day," Dag states as he bites into a peach. I guess fruit works when you're hungry enough. Suddenly, all three men tense.

Dane inclines his head, then he's standing. "Stay here," he orders

"What's wrong?" My heart is racing at the thought that there might be more danger.

"There is a man approaching," Eirik says just as someone rings the doorbell. I hear Dane opening the door and I can just imagine the poor man on the other side looking up at a mountain of a man like Dane. If he was here to hurt me, he will definitely think twice just by Dane's appearance alone.

"Yeah?" Dane's greeting is low, but I can still hear his threatening tone.

"Who are you?"

Recognising Kane's voice, I go to stand, but suddenly Eirik is standing next to my chair. Looking up at him he shakes his head.

"I'm none of your business, now what do you want?" I hear Dane ask once again impatiently.

"I know him, he co-stars with me."

Eirik just shrugs

"This is going to get interesting," Dag says with a grin

"Where is Freya?" I hear what sounds like a scuffle. "What do you think you doing?" Kane's voice is muffled as if Dane is cutting off his air supply.

"Dane, I know him," I call out, hoping that Dane will consider letting Kane go. Not that I mind him roughing Kane up a little as he's one of those obnoxious individuals that think that women can't live without them.

"I'll sue you for this," I hear Kane whingeing before I see him standing in the doorway. "Freya, what the hell is going on here?"

"Hi, Kane," I say conversationally as if this is an everyday occurrence. It's a good thing I put my contacts in when I left my room, or Kane is the type that would quickly tell everyone about my freaky eyes. "I believe you have met Dane. This here," I motion my head towards Eirik that is still standing next to me. "Is Eirik and that is Dag. They are my security detail." I see Kane's eyes widen as he looks over the men. Not being the most handsome man in the room must be upsetting him.

"Why didn't I get security detail?" His petulant voice is as irritating as usual. He's the most selfish, self-centred man I've ever met.

"Well, maybe it's because you weren't the one being threatened," I say. "What can I do for you?" I know it's rude to continue sitting while a guest is standing, but it looks like Eirik isn't going to let me go over to Kane. Not that it would make a difference because by the way Dane is glaring at him, I swear he will combust at any moment.

"I thought we could go through our scenes." Great, the last thing I feel like doing is spending a couple of hours with Kane, but one thing about him is that he's meticulous when it comes to his work. Sighing, I pull back my chair and stand.

"Fine, we can do it in the sitting room," I mutter,

wishing to spend time with Dane instead of rehearsing lines with Kane.

"Great," he says before glancing at Dane. "Maybe place your dogs on a leash."

"Fucker," Dag growls, quickly standing. His fast movement has my feet moving, walking around Eirik towards Kane, but it's too late because Dane has his arm around Kane's neck.

"You want to repeat what you just said?" Instead of repelling me, Dane's anger excites me. I like a man that isn't scared of standing up for himself or for those close to him. Kane was out of line and I completely support Dane in teaching him a lesson.

"Was a... fucking joke," Kane gasps as I raise my hand to place it on Dane's tense bicep.

His eyes are slitted in anger when he turns to look at me.

"Please let him go, he was just being an ass." Kane opens his mouth to respond, but I hold up my hand. "I would shut up if I were you," I warn, because I now have no doubt that Dane has no problem in ending someone's life.

"Thank you," I say when he drops his hand and steps between Kane and me. I place my hands flat on his back, feeling the muscles there rippling. I notice that he isn't wearing his kutte, only the black T-shirt he had on earlier, which has me thinking about his tattooed back, and how it rippled when he took off his T-shirt.

"Dane, we need to actually be together to go through the lines," I inform him. It's sweet how he's standing in front of me so protectively.

Dane grunts in annoyance before he takes a step to my side. "Touch her and you are dead."

Kane looks at me in surprise and then back at Dane.

"Well, that is going to be difficult because I have to kiss her for..." Dane has his hand around Kane's neck before he has a chance to finish his sentence. He pushes him forcefully against the wall, so hard that I'm sure he dented it.

"Dane," I call but he doesn't seem to be listening.

Dag and Eirik are suddenly pushing me out of the way as they try to get Dane's hand away from Kane's neck. Oh, my word, he wasn't joking. He will really kill any man that touches me. My heart is racing when I see how difficult it is for the men to pull Dane back.

"Dane, please." I don't want him to get into trouble because of me. "I'll never speak to you again if you kill him." I can feel my eyes filling with tears.

Kane is gasping, his lips turning an unearthly blue. "You think you're going to touch my woman? You'll be dead before I let you touch her." Dane's voice is menacing, his whole-body is rippling with anger. Dag and Eirik are pushing him back and it doesn't even seem like he feels them. He's a scary image indeed, standing here ready to kill a man for voicing that he was going to kiss me.

Walking behind him I place my hands on his back. "Please, Dane, you are worrying me." My voice is low, but I know that he can hear the worry in it. When I think my plea had no sway with him, he suddenly let's go of Kane.

DANE 5

The minute I let go of Kane's neck, Dag is pushing him out the door just in case I change my mind. I sure feel like killing the fucker for thinking that he is going to kiss Freya with the pretext of work. Well, if her work entails that motherfucker putting his hands anywhere near her, then she is going to change professions.

"Are you mad? Why would you nearly kill him?" Freya seems so distraught she has tears streaming down her cheeks. My heart tightens at her obvious distress. Fuck, what kind of mate am I when I put her in distress like this?

"He wanted to kiss you."

"That's part of the movie; it's not a real kiss."

"Really? Explain to me then what other kiss there is that doesn't involve him putting his lips on you?" Fury is coursing through my body when I think about the fucker coming anywhere near Freya. I slam my fist into the wall next to her, causing her to jump in surprise.

"It doesn't mean anything. It's just pretend."

"Listen to me, Freya. No man, pretend or not, is going to touch you." I know that I'm being hard on her, but she needs to understand that I will not have any other man near her.

"You are being bull-headed," she huffs angrily with her hands planted firmly on her waist. Fuck, she's beautiful when she's angry. Placing my other hand flat on the wall next to her head, I lean forward, caging her in between my arms.

"You belong to me—mine. No other fucker will touch you." I capture her lips in a blistering kiss. She will know what belonging to me feels like. She will want no lips except mine when I'm done with her. I feel her fist punching my chest in frustration before her hand slips up around my neck.

"There's a room just down the corridor," Dag quips from behind me, which has me flipping him off. Lifting my head, I glance over my shoulder to glare at him for the disruption. He shows me his phone. "Garth contacted me."

I know that when Dag went after the car that threw the brick through the window, he contacted Garth with a plate number. Garth must have found the culprit.

"You want to head out?" I ask, knowing that there must be a name for him to interrupt us.

"Yeah, I think you need some fresh air." If he only knew how right he is because if I stay here any longer, I will have Freya's legs around my waist, and I will be buried deep within her body before she even realizes it.

"Fine. I'll be out in a minute." Dag nods before turning to make his way out of the house.

"Eirik?" I call, knowing that he will look after Freya like she was his own mate, but I still need to confirm.

"Yeah."

I nod my thanks, looking back at Freya to see a curious expression.

"Be good. I'll be back soon." I lower my head down to kiss her, but she turns her head away from me at the last minute. My hand snaps to her jaw, turning her head so she is looking directly at me. "What?"

"You think you can kiss me, and I'll just forget that you

nearly killed a man," she whispers, her eyes snapping upward.

"But I didn't, so all is good," I mutter as I let go of her jaw. I turn to leave, but her hand on my arm stops me.

"Try not to kill anyone else, okay?" I can see a flicker of worry in her eyes before she looks down.

"Are you worried about me, sweet cakes?" My question has her eyes lifting back up to mine before she huffs and walks back to the table where we were sitting at earlier. Her show of worry has me grinning as I make my way outside towards my bike where Dag is waiting for me.

"Looks like you're in a better mood," Dag quips with a raised brow as he leans forward to start his bike.

"So, what do we know?" I ask, ignoring his previous comment.

"Garth ran the number plates. Apparently, the car belongs to a Mr. Fredrickson."

"Is there any connection?" Who the hell is this Fredrickson, and why does he want to hurt Freya?

"No, unless Freya didn't do an assignment." When Dag sees my confused scowl, he grins. "Apparently, this Fredrickson is a teacher."

"Well, let's go see what he has against my woman." He

better hope that I like his answers because I'm not taking too kindly to the idea of him wanting to hurt Freya. We make our way towards where this motherfucker lives. I follow Dag, already wishing I was back at the house with Freya. I know that as a mated couple, we miss each other's energy when we are apart, but I never thought we could feel the separation this soon after being with the other.

I've always been protective of others, especially women and children, but the feeling of protectiveness that I have towards my woman is so much more than that. I feel a strong need to have her close and make sure that she is out of harm's way. The possessiveness is new to me, as I've never been possessive about much except for my motorcycle. To know that someone wants Freya harmed, has all kinds of feelings that I'm not used to, messing with me.

We approach a quiet suburban area. What the fuck would anyone living in a suburb like this want with Freya? The roads are quiet as we drive through before Dag pulls up to a house. There are no cars in the driveway, but we walk up to the door anyway, hearing noises inside. The vehicles are probably in the double door garage next to the house.

Dag rings the bell. I would kick the fucking door in, but I don't think Tor would be too pleased with me. A man in his late fifties opens the door. The surprise on his face is comical when he sees the two of us standing on the other side. If I wasn't pissed, I would probably find it funny because he probably thinks we are here to rob him.

"Umm, can I help you?"

"Are you Mr. Fredrickson?" The man looks surprised at Dag's question, but he nods. "Do you own a blue Ford?"

"Yes, what is this about?" There is a hesitation when Dag asks him if he owns the blue Ford, which leads me to believe that there is more to this story than what meets the eye.

"Someone driving that vehicle threw a brick through my woman's window."

I can see the surprise and anger on Mr. Fredrickson's face, which tells me that it wasn't him.

"I'm so sorry. Was anyone hurt?" he asks.

"Who was driving the vehicle, Mr. Fredrickson?"

Dag's question has him hesitating before he answers. "My son drives that car. He is just a teenager and in a rebellious phase. I will pay for any damages that his actions have acquired."

I take a step forward, which has him taking a step back. "We want to speak to your son." I can see the worry on his face. He probably thinks that we are going to hurt his son, and I might still, if the asshole becomes cocky. I really just want to frighten the kid, so he learns never to do that again, and to know if anyone put him up to it.

"Why?"

"There have been threats made against my woman. We want to know if your kid knows anything about it."

The man pales before he starts shaking his head. "My son's rebellious, but he's not a criminal. He wouldn't go to those lengths." He glances over his shoulder and then back at us. "You're not going to hurt him, are you?"

"No, but I think he needs a fright, maybe get him over his rebellion."

I can see he's hesitant, but he nods, turning his back on us.

"Craig," he calls.

"What?"

"There are two gentlemen here to see you." Dag elbows me and grins, mouthing the word *'Gentlemen'*. I shake my head at his strange sense of humour just as Craig walks towards the door, I can see a surprised look on his face and then he is looking behind him hesitantly as if he's thinking about bolting. Stupid kid, I'll catch him before he gets away, but he thinks better of it as he steps up next to his father.

"Umm, yeah?"

"You know why we are here?" Dag asks with a raised brow at him, I simply fold my arms and stare, waiting.

He looks at us cautiously as he shrugs, then glances at his father before looking at us again. "No idea."

Fuck, the last thing I want is to shake down a kid but if he won't talk. I'm not taking a chance with my woman's life.

"You threw a brick through someone's window," the dad suddenly says. "Why would you do that?"

At his fathers' accusation, he tenses, his expression clearly guilty. "Some woman paid us to do it."

I grunt. A woman is threatening Freya? "Do you know who she is?" I ask, only to receive another shrug from him.

"Didn't you ask her any questions when she offered you money to go and vandalize someone's property?" I swear if he doesn't start talking soon, I'm going to peg him up to the door.

"No. She offered us one hundred dollars to just throw a brick through someone's window. We didn't ask any questions." I can imagine that for a teenager that doesn't know anything about exchange rate when someone offers him dollars instead of our current rand currency, he probably thinks he's getting rich.

"Where is the money?" the father asks with an angry scowl on his face

"It's my money." I've had enough of his belligerent behaviour. I've never been one for patience, and I'm not going to start now. Snapping my hand forward, I grab him by the neck, pulling him close until he is nose-to-nose with me. I hear his father's intake of breath, but to his credit he doesn't interfere.

"Now listen here. You threw a brick through my woman's window." His eyes fill with widening fear. "If someone was in the kitchen at the time, you could have hurt them. You will pay for that window and you will tell us everything you know about her if you want to carry on breathing." He nods vigorously, I can smell his fear. My phone starts to vibrate in my pocket, but I ignore it. We need information on who paid these kids to frighten Freya, and if this kid can give us any information, then I'm not leaving here until I know everything.

"Tell us what the woman looked like," Dag asks as he places a hand on my shoulder, squeezing lightly so that I take a step back.

"Don't know. Looked like a rich chick," the kid says with a shrug. "She was wearing fancy shoes and smelled of really strong perfume."

"Anything you can tell us about how she looks?" Dag asks

"I don't know. She was hot with an American accent." My phone starts to vibrate again.

Fuck. Taking a step back, I pull it out of my pocket.

"Yeah?"

"What the fuck do you think you were doing?" Tor's voice rumbles down the line.

"What?"

"I just had a fucking call from Mr. Taylor telling me that you nearly killed one of his actors." The anger in his voice is tangible. Shit, that's all I need right now is Tor on my case. "Why the fuck would you be threatening an actor? Do you know that he wants to file charges against you?"

"It's fine, I'll go speak to him," I mumble. Maybe that will get him off my back.

"You aren't going anywhere near him again; do you understand me, Dane?" There is a threat in his voice that I would do good not to ignore. Tor guides us with a strong arm, but there is no better man to be at our side than him. He will give up his life for anyone of us and we would do the same. Even though we aren't the mellow, follow every order kind of guys, we do appreciate strength, and, in our chapter, there is no one stronger than Tor.

"Yeah,"

"Also, there seems to be more activity from The Desperados street gang. I want you three to keep an eye open for anything new."

"Will do," I say, thinking back to the Desperados that Eirik saw when we left the hotel this morning.

"We are on our way back and should be back in Cape Town tomorrow." Tor, Tal, Asger and Colborn had a weapons shipment to collect from the Johannesburg chapter and were delivering it to the client before coming back, I guess they have finalized the delivery and are returning. The Elementals main source of income comes from smuggling weapons into Africa, but as a cover, we have various other businesses such as this security gig that Tor is so protective of.

"Are you sure that is all you know?" I hear Dag ask as I disconnect the call.

"Yeah," the kid replies.

"If I find out that you are keeping something from us. We will be back and then you'll be sorry because next time I will let my friend here take his frustration out on you."

Just for effect, I scowl at him, which has the kid taking a step back. "That is all I know," The kid states.

Dag looks at me and inclines his head towards the bikes, and I'm more than happy to leave.

"Did we get anything?" I ask as we sit on our bikes,

"No. Only that it was a woman that looked rich with strong perfume and bleached blond hair."

"Fuck, do you think it's a woman sending the threats?" Dag shrugs as he leans over his bike to start it.

"By the way, Tor wants us to keep an eye out for Desperados." Dag nods before he pulls away from Frederickson's house. I follow behind him, glad to be going back to Freya.

FREYA 6

"He was just being overprotective, Kane. I've had threats made against me and that's why." When Tom phoned to tell me that Kane was filing charges against Dane, I convinced Eirik to accompany me here to try to change his mind. I know that he will be an ass and make me beg. He has always been full of himself. If he sees that this will bring him publicity, he will milk it to its last reserve.

"He knew I wasn't a threat, look..." He steps closer, showing me his neck. "I have his fingers all over my neck."

"A little concealer will cover those," I assure him, but looking at the bruises, I wish I could punch Dane for the hassle he is giving me. "If you lay a charge, then everyone will think that you were trying to attack me. Is that what you want people to think?"

A look of shock crosses his face. "Why would they think that?" I need to play my cards right or Dane might be arrested for this.

"Well, my security detail detained you by force. What does that look like?"

"But I wasn't doing anything," he says angrily, his blue eyes flashing with rage.

"But no one knows that. You do know how people like to invent things and all you need to do is give them a gap and they will be thinking weird things about you."

He huffs in anger as he snaps around to look at Tom, who is sitting on the couch, watching the two of us.

"You need to do something," Kane says as he goes to stand before Tom with his hand on his waist.

"I've spoken to their boss. He will be in tomorrow to speak to me," Tom states.

I really hope this isn't going to get Dane into trouble. What will happen to him if his boss is angry? I don't think the term boss applies in this situation, as I don't think the Elementals have bosses.

"This can't stay like this," Kane whines. He is so petty that I really wish I never have to work with him again.

My heart is racing at the thought of Dane going to jail for this. For some reason, the thought of not being able to be with Dane has me stressing. I know that this situation I'm in is strange beyond anything I would ever have imagined, but I've always been someone that follows their instinct, and my instincts are screaming that everything Dane said is true. How can I doubt it when I have this tattoo on my arm that I'm currently hiding under my shirt? It's proof that things beyond what we know do exist.

I feel at home with Dane, and even though he is completely out of my comfort zone, I know that I won't find happiness with anyone else like Dane will be able to give me. My body still tingles when I think about how he feels in my body—how it feels when he kisses me.

"Freya?"

I glance at Tom, realizing that he must have said something that I completely missed when I was distracted thinking about Dane. "Yes?"

He raises a brow in question but doesn't berate me like is his habit. "I was saying," he says with a pointed look at me, "that your security detail will stay away from Kane, and that the man that attacked him will stay away from the studio." Now this is something that I can agree to because I like that I can finish my set without Dane threatening mayhem on anyone that comes too close.

"Sure." I glance over my shoulder at Eirik, who is standing by the door. He raises a brow at me, as if saying good luck. "Actually, I think that Eirik will be the one accompanying me from now on into the studio."

Eirik's expression doesn't change, but I do notice that his body has tensed.

"Good. You don't, perchance have a desire for strangling people, do you?"

Eirik glances at Tom, but then looks away again without a reply.

"You see how rude they are?" Kane mutters as he shakes his head.

"Well, they are the best at what they do," Tom states as he stands. "Now, if this has been resolved, can we please get on with more important things?"

"Well, I'm sorry, but I tend to think that my life is important," Kane whines as he whips around to make his way out of the room.

"He'll be back," Tom sighs, shaking his head. We all know Kane loves his hissy fits and when he has calmed, he walks back in as if nothing happened. Tom points at me. "You haven't signed the new contract yet."

"I'm still thinking."

A great opportunity has come up for me to be a lead in a motion picture, but I've been holding onto deciding from the moment Tom gave me the contract two weeks ago. I know it's a great opportunity, and the money will be amazing, but I've been questioning my options for a while now. I became an actress by chance. One day I was serving drinks on a plane to a producer, and the next I'm in his movie.

At the time I was blown away by the money and the attention, but as time went by, I became aware that I wasn't happy. I'm more isolated than ever before. I can't make friends because I don't trust anyone, and I can't afford for anyone to find out about my secret because it would blow up in my face. The lack of freedom has also been a big thing for me, I've always loved nature and the fact that I can't go out for a walk because I might be accosted by fans, has diminished the glamour of this occupation.

"We need to send it back. What is wrong?" I can hear the exasperation in his voice.

"I'm just not sure this is what I want," I say with a shrug.

"This is what everyone wants. How can you even be hesitant?" The irritation in his voice is evident.

"Maybe it's just not what I want."

He stands, taking an angry step towards me before he stops. "What is this about? Do you want more money?"

Gosh no. The role is already paying more than enough.

"I want more freedom. I can't do anything, Tom." I throw up my hands in exasperation. "Everywhere I go, people know me."

"You can do anything you want. You have money. You have the resources to do more than the average person. So yes, people might know you wherever you go, but that's a good thing in your profession." He will never understand because he loves the attention and having people around him. In my case, I would rather be incognito. "You have two more weeks under this contract, then all the interviews and marketing that comes with it. You will have four months off before you need to start filming again. In those four months, you can do anything you want, go anywhere you want, and no one will bug you." That's just the problem, I can't because everywhere I go, people seem to recognize me.

"I'll get the contract back to you by Monday." I don't promise the contract will be signed because I really don't think I can do this any longer. I haven't got any friends, my mother hardly speaks to me, and I'm alone. All the money in the world doesn't make me happy when I've got no one to share it with. Now that I have Dane, I want to make a life for myself—one that I'll be happy with and not just living day to day.

"Good girl. Now off you go, I have a few calls to make."

I nod, more than happy to leave. Eirik walks to the door,

opening it so he can look out before standing aside to let me pass.

"Oh, and Freya," Tom calls just before I step out, "make sure you leave the other security detail outside or Kane might decide to quit." For some reason, I think it's easier said than done, but I agree before leaving with Eirik walking out right beside me.

"Dane's not going to like it, is he?"

"Nope," Eirik replies without a glance at me.

"Will you accompany me, though?" I ask, and this time I have him stop and look directly at me.

"This isn't a job for us any longer, sweetheart. You belong to one of us, and for that, we will always be there to protect you no matter what. Dane as your mate should be the one to protect you, but because of his temper, he will have to understand. It was good of you to intervene and stop that fucker from filing charges against Dane." Eirik lifts his hand and I see that he has his phone in it. Looking down, he inclines his head towards the front doors. "Speak of the devil, looks like Dane is outside."

I tense. *How the hell did he know we were here?*

"Did you tell him where we were?" I ask, turning to hurry down the corridor to the main door.

"No. But as his mate, he will always be able to find you

no matter where you are."

Oh great, another thing I didn't know about this relationship. It's like having a tracker up your ass.

"Can I do that, find him wherever he is?"

Eirik shakes his head, a grin transforming his formidable expression.

"Oh, I don't see that being very fair, now is it?"

He shrugs, his grin widening further. Eirik opens the door for me to walk out. I see Dane and Dag sitting on their bikes just a couple of feet away. When I see him, it feels like all my anxiety just washes away.

"I didn't think you were working today?" Dane says when we stop next to the bikes.

"I wasn't, but I came in to speak to Tom."

I see Dane raise his head and then he tenses. His eyes get intense when he turns to Eirik. "And that fucker, too?"

How the hell did he know that?

"They just spoke. She got him to drop the charges against you."

"How do you know I spoke to him?" Dane looks back at me, his features still tense.

"I can smell the son of a bitch." Oh, my goodness, how am I supposed to do the scenes tomorrow if he can smell when I'm close to Kane? I look over at Eirik and see a splitting grin across his face. He is enjoying this and I can tell he knows exactly what I'm thinking.

"You know a thank you would be nice," I growl, still upset with the fact that I have no idea how I'm going to film the sets that still need to be filmed without Dane killing Kane for touching me.

Suddenly, Dane is grabbing my upper arm and pulling me closer to him as he continues sitting on the bike. "I don't want you to ever put yourself in a situation where you need to save me from anything," he whispers before his head lowers, and he's kissing me senseless.

"Well, well, what is this?" I break the kiss, my head snapping around to see Tanya standing a few feet away with an irritating and content expression on her face. "Slumming it, I see." I sense the anger radiating from the men at her comments. Turning, I face Tanya, wanting to slap the shit out of her sarcastic smile.

"Hi, Tanya. Jealous?"

"Well, honey, they are hot, but I never thought you would fall so low for attention." I hear a whoosh, glancing back I see Dane is off his bike, his shoulders wide behind me.

"Listen here, lady..."

I turn, gently placing my hand on his chest. "Don't bother," I soothe him. "Shall we go?" I can tell that Dane would like nothing more than to put Tanya in her place, but Tanya has been picking on me from the moment our filming started. I have no doubt that she won't stop just because Dane says something to her. Dane looks down at me, his features strained, but he must see something in my expression that has him nod.

"You are with me." He picks up a helmet that is on his handlebars and helps me put it on. I've never been on a motorcycle before; coming here, we took my rental, and I was thinking of going back in it, but I guess Eirik will be driving it back alone. To be honest, I'm excited. I've always wanted to go on a bike, and now it's my chance.

"What about you?" I see Dane doesn't have a helmet; I must be wearing his.

"I'll be fine, don't worry," he says with a boyish grin. I hear Tanya something, but none of us are listening to her. Dag has already started his bike, and Eirik is making his way towards the rental just as Dane helps me on the bike behind him. "Hold on," he says as he pulls my arms around him, so my hands are flat against his abdomen. My breasts push against his back, and I feel the warmth of his leather kutte, and all the muscles rippling under it as he starts his bike.

Just before we pull away, I glance towards Tanya and

see her taking a photo with her phone. The expression on her face is the same expression I've seen many times before when she is up to no good, and I know that whatever it is, I'm not going to like it.

The minute Dane pulls onto the street, my arms tighten around him when I feel the wind blowing around me, but soon I relax as a sense of freedom washes over me. The only thing that I sense is the wind whipping around me, and Dane's protection warming everything inside of me. *Why haven't I done this before?*

"I love this!" I shout, knowing Dane has heard me when his hand touches one of mine and he squeezes it gently. I've had more excitement in the last day than I've had most of my life. I have a feeling that every day with Dane will be a new experience. He has a temper that is triggered by the smallest things. I don't know how he has made it this long without being sent away to jail for life. But whatever the reason, I'm thankful for the fact that I've met him, and that I'm his mate.

DANE 7

"Tor is on his way," Dag says as he walks into the kitchen.

"Shit," I snap, my fingers threading through my hair.

"Hey, at least he let you have a good night's sleep," Dag quips with a wink which has me raising my hand to show him my middle finger. Freya is still sleeping; I know she will be tired today, I made sure she never doubts who she belongs to. To be honest, I'm a little tired myself, but damn I feel good. Not even Tor will bring me down today.

Just then Eirik walks in. He was out the whole night trying to figure out what the Desperados are up to.

"Anything?" I ask.

"Yeah, but I need coffee first." Dag lifts the jug as Eirik opens the cupboard for a mug. "Those fuckers are looking for Sean's woman, apparently she's missing." Sean is The Desperados leader; he is a mean son of a bitch. If the woman has gone missing, it must mean that she has run away.

"I didn't know Sean had only one woman," Dag mutters as he takes a sip of his coffee

"Apparently he doesn't have just one, but this one was his favourite, and from what our source said, she ran away with something valuable that Sean wants back."

"That means he will most probably kill her when he finds her. You know that bastard holds nothing sacred except money."

Eirik pulls out a photo from his pocket, placing it on the table. "Apparently that's her." In the photo is a woman with big, wide green eyes, and she's investigating the camera as her hair floats around her. There is a haunted look to her that has a protective instinct rise in me. This woman is clearly not happy.

"Fuck," Dag's angry word has me looking at him to see his eyes glued to the photo.

"Do you know her?" Eirik asks with a frown

"I don't know, but I feel a fucking urgency to find her."

He picks up the photo, his finger stroking her face gently as if caressing her very skin. I glance over my shoulder when I sense Freya approaching. When she walks into the kitchen, everything around me seems to still. This woman has turned everything I consider normal, and is now filling my life with a new reality that I never knew existed, but that I'm more than willing to experience.

"Good Morning." Her voice is still husky. All my senses are instantly on alert. My cock hardens at her presence. Fuck, I don't know how it even has the energy after last night.

"I'm surprised your face hasn't cracked," Eirik teases, which has me winking at him just as I hear bikes approaching. "Looks like your smile is going to end quick."

Standing, I approach Freya. She has plaited her hair, her eyes still heavy from lack of sleep. I'm surprised that she is even awake. Placing my hand behind her neck, I pull her forward.

"Oh," she murmurs in surprise, her hands lifting to my chest while her eyes soften as she looks at my lips.

"You're about to meet some more of our guys, and Tor. He is the Cape Town Elementals Chapter President." Her eyes widen in surprise just as I kiss her lips. I would rather my woman's mind be all on me when she meets the others. When I finally lift my head, her heart rate is accelerated, her breathing laboured, and I know that she wants me again.

Eirik walks towards the door as I guide Freya over to the kitchen table, helping her into one of the chairs just as Tor walks in with Garth, Tal and Asgar right behind him. It's evident that the extra day has done nothing for Tor's mood.

"Guys."

Tor grunts as he comes to stand before Freya and me, his eyes roving over the two of us.

"Nice to meet you, Freya."

I notice her smiling at Tor, which has me frowning. Tor has a way about him. He's a sweet talker with woman and can make them do anything he wants.

"Freya, this is Tor, our Chapter President."

"I hear that you stopped this fool from being arrested?" Tor says as he pulls out a chair and takes a seat.

"It was nothing," she says with a smile, but I can see that her hands are fisted in her lap. Placing my hand over hers, I squeeze gently, knowing that she feels overwhelmed with so many men in the kitchen.

"Freya, that there is Asgar." Asgar glances over his shoulder at us and nods. "And this is Garth and Tal."

"You look just like in your movie," Tal says with a wink.

"Damn, are you sure you want Dane? I'm available."

"In your dreams, Tal," I say, knowing that he's teasing, but not liking it.

"From what I was told, I don't have a choice?" Freya says looking at me.

"You don't," I state.

"How about telling me what the fuck you were thinking about when you attacked that actor?" Tor suddenly asks, his expression now hard as he stares at me.

"He fucking wanted to kiss Freya." Tor glances at Freya then back at me, his expression unchanged.

"I knew mates were a fucking problem," he grumbles as he closes his eyes for a few seconds before lifting his hand to rub his unshaven jaw. "Mine better stay far away for as long as possible."

There was a time that Tor thought he had found his mate, but one of the women had a gift of manipulating people. Because of Tor's glib tongue, she decided she wanted to teach him a lesson, so she manipulated his feelings to the point where he thought she was his mate. Once she realized that she was way over her head, she stopped her manipulation. Needless to say, Tor has been on a rampage against mates ever since. Soraya, the woman that manipulated his feelings, is now mated to another Elemental, but Tor is still sore about the fact that she played him.

When he found out that Soraya was mated, we all thought he was going to blow up after what happened. Yes, he was upset, but nowhere as upset as we thought he would have been.

"Fuck, Tor, don't say that. We need a woman to keep you occupied," Garth says as he leans against the door.

"I have more than enough woman keeping me occupied," Tor grunts. "Now what have we found out about The Desperados, why are they all over town?" Dag pulls the photo out of his inside kutte pocket, passing it to Tor.

"They are looking for that woman. Apparently, she belongs to Sean," Dag says, but there's an angry note in his voice.

"Her name is Esmeralda, and she took something that Sean wants back," Eirik says with a shrug.

"Esmeralda?" Dag asks, there is a strange note in his voice that has Tor raise a brow at him. "We need to find her before one of his goons do, you know what will happen if he gets her back."

"Why the concern for this woman?" Tor asks

"I don't know, but I know that we need to try find her," Dag says as he runs his fingers through his hair. In Dag's case, that is a sign of stress. Why would Dag be stressed about this woman?

"Fuck Dag, she better not be yours," Tor mutters. "Speaking of that, what is your gift Freya?" At Tor's question, I realize that Freya and I never got to finish our conversation. I feel Freya stiffen beside me, which has me pulling my hand from on top of hers so I can I throw my arm over her shoulder and bring her closer to me.

"Umm." She glances at me before she bites her bottom lip in indecision. "I can freeze people without them knowing."

What the fuck does she mean, freeze people?

"What does that mean?" Tor asks with a scowl.

"It means that usually when I get stressed, I can stop people or things for a couple of minutes."

"You mean time?" Tal asks as he comes to stand behind Tor.

"Yes, you could say that."

My woman can stop time?

"But time doesn't really stop, only people or things. I've been able to stop a car before."

"How do you go about doing that?" Garth asks.

Freya shrugs with a frown. "I say stop."

"And can you just stop one person or everyone around that person?" I ask.

"I've only done it when there is one person around. I've never tried to direct it to only one person in a group or to a group."

Tor looks at me, inclining his head towards Freya. "Figure it out," he states as he pulls the chair back. " I need to meet with your agent. Anything I need to know?" Tor asks Freya.

"Yes. He agreed to let everything run as is, if Dane stays away from the set."

My back straightens. It's the first I'm hearing about this. "Fuck no." There is no way I'm letting Freya back on set without me. Whoever wants to harm her is one of her colleagues, I'm nearly one hundred percent sure of that.

"You messed it up. So you stay behind and someone else will go with your woman." The thought of her being on set near that fucker, or in danger has my whole-body straining.

"Tor. . ." I start to argue, but he interrupts me.

"Don't argue. You nearly cost us this security gig. I had to listen to the agent ranting on the phone for fifteen fucking minutes, and then the organizer, which I have an agreement with, also phoned in to complain. So, you will trust the others to look after your woman and you will grin and bear it."

Fuck, I know that tone, it's Tor's tone when he won't budge from his decision. I just wish Freya had told me before about this agreement she did with her fucking agent.

I nod, letting Tor know that I agree, but I will fucking make sure that whoever goes with Freya keeps me informed of everything, twenty-four seven.

"Do you have any idea who is threatening Freya?" Garth asks, which has Dag explaining about our meeting with the kid yesterday.

When Dag finishes his recounting, Tor stands. "Eirik, you and Garth are with Freya today. Dane, you go with Dag and see if you can find this woman the Desperados are after. Asgar you're with me. We have to meet with the Agent."

My mind won't be on finding this fucking woman that Dag is so desperate to save. I would rather be with my mate. Fuck, I swear I should have killed that son of a bitch that thought he could kiss Freya. Then I wouldn't have this problem. With my arm around Freya's shoulders, I pull her closer to me, kissing the top of her head. "Be good today," I murmur, which has her glancing up at me and shrugging.

"I'm always good." I have a feeling that she is, but it's the men around her that I don't trust.

"Let's go, Brother," Dag calls from the door

"Why the hell are you in such a hurry? It's not like we even know where to start," I ask as I lower my head to kiss Freya's lips gently before standing. On my way out, I look at Eirik. "Keep me updated," I order in passing, but I know that he heard me and knows exactly what I'm talking about. I've only been with my mate for a short time, but I already feel the change in me. I know that she will make me a better person and I will want to be better for her, but I think until that happens, she will have to be patient with me because I know I can be hot headed and explosive—a combination that isn't easy to live with.

FREYA 8

"Eirik," I sigh in exasperation, but he just raises a brow with a straight face. I know he's enjoying this. "You can't stand here while we shoot."

"I'm staying here." There is no doubt by his tone that he's not changing his mind.

"Okay, please don't make a noise." He nods but doesn't say anything as his eyes continue to look around the area. "And, Eirik, please don't interrupt us if Kane touches me, it is part of the scene."

"You know that Dane is not going to be happy about that, don't you?"

"I know," I grumble as I pull the small skirt down, trying to cover more of my thighs. I swear the skirt got smaller since the last time I wore it.

"You are a clever one. That is why you arranged that Garth and I keep an eye on you instead of your mate." Darn, I never expected him to catch onto my plan.

"Yes."

"Well, let me tell you, that if Dane senses that any man has touched you, he will kill him and there is nothing you can do."

I gasp at his words. "Don't say that." I raise my hand to my chest, feeling my heart race in anxiety. "In this scene, Kane kisses me. It is part of this shot."

"Well, he better enjoy it because it will be the last kiss of his life," Eirik states with a shrug.

"Can't you keep him away from Kane until tomorrow midday?" I hope he can, because if he can't, the only thing I can do is hide from Dane until Kane is gone.

"You have seen Dane; do you think that it will be easy to stop him if he really wants to do something?"

"Different one today, I see." Tanya's sarcastic comment has me stilling. I glance over my shoulder as she walks past. "Looks like the little librarian has a taste for bikers."

"You want me to shut her up?" Eirik asks in a menacing tone that has Tanya hurriedly walking away. "I really don't like that woman," he growls, which has me smiling. It's the first time Eirik shows any semblance of being irritated.

"No, it's okay. You know that karma has a way of biting back."

His expression doesn't change, but he nods, his eyes still on Tanya that is now standing by the producer.

"Are you ready?" Looking at Janine, I smile. Time to maybe get Kane killed. Taking a deep breath, I turn and make my way towards set. We start filming, my mind is everywhere, but somehow, I make it through my lines and from what the producer says it seems like he likes them, then it's the kissing scene and I can feel my heart racing, my palms are perspiring, and I feel such a nauseating feeling in the pit of my stomach that I swear I will get sick if Kane kisses me.

"What the hell is wrong with you?" Kane whispers as he steps into place.

"I'm not feeling well," I breathe.

"Well, make sure you keep it together until we are finished. I need to get this wrapped up today." Kane doesn't think about anyone but himself, but the one thing I'm in total agreement with is that the sooner we finish, the sooner he will be gone and out of harm's way—Dane's way.

I stand in position waiting for the producer to give us the go ahead. My stomach is heaving at the thought of Kane kissing me, but it needs to be done. Maybe I'll just change it slightly, instead of him kissing me I'll push him away before his lips can touch mine. After all, it is supposed to happen; I'll just make it more believable by slapping him. When I hear action I automatically go into my role, forgetting everything and everyone around me and becoming one with my character. When Kane starts to lean towards me, I raise my hand and slap him across the face.

His eyes widen in surprise as I say my lines.

Luckily, he catches on and quickly composes himself by saying his own lines. I can see the anger in his eyes but the producer hasn't stopped us so he must be happy with the scene. The day drags on, but finally it's time to stop. Taking a deep breath, I turn to make my way towards my dressing room. I just want to go home, have a hot bath, and relax.

I'm nearly by my dressing room when I suddenly see Eirik walking towards me. By the expression on his face, I can tell that he isn't happy. "Don't even think about it."

Eirik's threat has me glancing back over my shoulder just in time to see Kane, his hand raised as if to grab my arm. At Eirik's statement he stops, dropping his hand.

The glare he throws Eirik doesn't seem to faze him as he comes to stand behind me. Eirik's wide back is blocking out Kane, which in a way I really don't mind as I've had more than enough of him today. "What? Can't I talk to her?"

I sigh as I turn around and step to the side to see Kane. "What's wrong, Kane?"

"Why didn't you tell me that you were going to change the kissing scene? Did you think you would make a fool out of me by springing that on me?" He is so loud that the other actors who were standing nearby look over at us.

"No. I just wasn't feeling well like I told you, so I thought it was better doing that then getting sick all over you."

At my statement he huffs, but he seems to have run out of steam as he complains, "you need to communicate with your colleagues," before he turns and makes his way towards his changing room. Because of Kane leaving, we did all the scenes that were needed with him. Now the others shouldn't take as long.

"I'm just going to change, Eirik, I'll be right out," I announce as I walk into my changing room and close the door behind me. The quiet surrounds me. Taking in a deep breath, I shut my eyes for a minute before opening them again. Walking towards where Janine left my usual bottle of water, I uncap it, take a seat on the chair before the mirror, and take a sip of the cool water.

The best thing I like about shooting a scene is when I get to come back to the dressing room, away from everyone, and relax for a couple of minutes with my thoughts.

After drinking half the bottle of water, I sigh and start to get ready. I don't like making anyone wait for me. As I start towards the door, I feel such a strong cramp that I double over gasping. What the hell was that? Is this still because I mated with Dane? When I can finally walk again, I step carefully towards the door just in case it decides to hit me again.

"You ready?" I nod at Eirik's question, but I'm not feeling well at all. Is this my nerves thinking over if Dane will go after Kane? I can feel myself breakout in a cold sweat, and my vision is starting to blur. What the hell is wrong with me? We make our way to the car. Once inside, I lay my head back and close my eyes.

"Are you okay?" I hear Eirik's concern, but my eyes are too heavy for me to open them.

"I'm okay, only tired." I feel like all my energy is being depleted.

"I don't blame you; they are like a school of piranhas in there. I've never seen so many fake people in one room, like I did with that bunch." I try to smile at Eirik's displeased tone, from what I've gathered from being with the men for such a short time, is that they say what they mean. I doubt no one ever questions what their intentions are.

"Dane phoned earlier, wanted to know how you were doing. Are you going to tell him about Kane?"

I frown at Eirik's question.

"I thought he could tell when someone touched me?"

"Yes, he can, but as you know, he will want to kill him for the simple reason that he placed his hands on you. If he thinks that he kissed you, nothing will stop him from going after Kane."

I sigh, my head feeling woozy like I'm coming down with the flu, the last thing I feel like doing is thinking about this.

"It will be fine," I whisper.

"You don't seem too hot, sugar, are you sure you're okay?"

My legs feel so heavy, I don't know why I'm feeling so sick. "I'm just so tired," I murmur. My whole body is starting to feel heavy now.

"Freya, look at me!" I hear Eirik snap, but for the life of me I can't open my eyes, it feels like lead weights are pulling them down. "Freya!"

"Tired," I whisper.

"Dane, there's something wrong with your woman."

What? What's happening?

"I don't fucking know, but I think she was poisoned, Brother."

Poisoned? No, I'm fine. I'm just tired. I try to open my eyes again, but they won't open. Was I poisoned? Who would have done something like this to me? I know that there is a lot of rivalry on set, but surely no one would go this far. I can feel myself start to panic, but the more I try, the heavier I seem to be getting. I sense my consciousness start to slip. No... no, I can't be poisoned. I've just met Dane. I don't want to die like this.

"Freya, hang in there we're nearly home," I hear Eirik say as if he's far away. I know that I'm going to lose consciousness, and the only thing I can think about in this moment is that I didn't even get to see Dane one more time.

I must have passed out because the next thing I know, there is a roaring in my ears—thudding. What is making such a racket? Then it sounds like something rips followed by a grunt before silence again.

"Three days... three fucking days and nothing?" Dane's roar has me awakening from whatever poisoned stupor I'm in. But I still can't open my eyes. I try to move my fingers, but the pain that shoots through my muscles has me instantly stilling. How did they poison me?

"Calm the fuck down. You will be no good to your

woman if I have to knock you out."

Tor? What is Tor doing here?

"I know this is messing with your head, but now more than ever you need to keep your shit together because we need to catch who did this and make them pay." I feel the darkness try to pull me down again, but I fight it. I want to hear Dane's voice—feel his touch, but the darkness has no mercy and soon everything is going black again and silence is reigning.

Heat is what wakes me up. There's a burning sensation deep in my stomach. It feels like I'm burning from the inside out, then I feel a cool breeze on my face and the heat on my cheeks starts to cool. "She's still burning up. Shouldn't she be better by now?" The sound of Dane's voice has me calming, the heat starting to diminish. I feel Dane's hand in mine... wait... I can feel his hand. My heart starts to race, I try to open my eyes, and again, I find it difficult to lift them because of the heaviness, but at least I'm starting to feel everything around me.

"Bion just phoned earlier and promises me that the only thing I can do for her, is carry on giving her my blood and touching her as much as I can."

"Tor said the worst was behind you, and that she will start to get better now." *Whose voice is that? Doesn't sound like any of the men I've met before.* I'm curious to know who this voice belongs to. Its deep timbre has me calming. His voice seems to radiate peace which has my tense muscles relaxing. Only now do I realize that my muscles were taut, but more importantly, I'm feeling my body again. The heaviness that has been with me from the moment I started to feel ill is now gone.

I try to call out, but my throat feels so dry that at first nothing happens and then after another two tries I manage to croak out, "Dane."

The conversation that the two men were having suddenly stops.

"Freya?" There is a hesitant note in Dane's voice. "Can you hear me?" I want to nod, but my muscles still feel stiff and achy.

"Yes." The word is barely a whisper, but at least I'm communicating. I try to open my eyes, and this time they open just a slit, which has me still seeing everything in a blur.

"Here, take a sip of this," Dane slips a straw between my lips, the water burns my dry throat, but I'm so parched that I can't help myself but to drink it. His fingers are stroking my hair as I drink. "Slowly," he encourages. I just want to be able to open my eyes and see his face again, but instead of widening my vision, my eyes once again close. I feel like the weight of the world is on my shoulders. I'm so tired, but I know that the poison must be working its way out of my system, and hopefully soon, I will be back to myself and then I'll be able to look at Dane for as long as I like.

DANE 9

You would think that my anger would have calmed with Freya opening her eyes, but it hasn't. The molten fury that is coursing through my body over the fact that someone nearly killed Freya has been driving me crazy. I wasn't with her when she first fell ill, I will never let that happen again. This was all because of my quick temper. If I wasn't such a hot-headed asshole, I wouldn't have gone hunting with Dag for The Desperado's woman and would have been keeping an eye on my woman's welfare instead, making sure that she was kept safe.

When Eirik phoned me, I was already on my way back because I had a feeling that Freya wasn't well. I owe him an apology. I was out of my mind with worry for her and accused him of not paying attention, but I know that he would have done everything in his power to protect her. No one would have known that the poison was there. The bottle was closed. Tal and Haldor went back to the set to see what they could find. When they brought back the bottle, we realized that someone injected the poison into it because there was a needle prick on the lid.

We had to get a doctor. Luckily, Doctor Hendriks was close. He has been with us for a long time and keeps everything quiet. He doesn't do any tests and only treats wounds, or in this case, poisoning. But he wasn't helping because Freya was slipping away before my very eyes. Therefore, we called Bion one of the brothers in our Mother Chapter. He is one of our best healers. He insisted that the best thing for Freya was for me to give her more of my blood, as it will combat the poison and kick it out of her system.

It's been a hard couple of days, but now she has finally opened her eyes. Her agent was insisting that we take her to a hospital, but Tor convinced him to leave her with us, and assured him she was getting all the best care possible. We brought her back to the club after the first day. Word got out about her poisoning and we had reporters phoning and camping outside the door, waiting for news. The last thing we need is eyes on us.

They will find more than they bargained for if they start snooping into the Elementals MC business.

"She will be fine." Asgar brings me back from my thoughts with his words.

"Yeah." Looking at him by the door, I see his eyes on me. Their penetrating intensity tells me that he is analysing the situation. Asgar is a great strategist, as he will analyse a situation to exhaustion before committing himself.

"I was thinking," he says as he rubs his jaw.

"Of course, you were," I quip. We all tease him about overthinking things.

He ignores my words as he continues. "There are only two women on set that are suspects. The man has left, so there is no further suspicion there." The mention of the man has me scowling, as I remember when I first got to Freya and how I sensed Kane. I know she was working, and that she had to shoot scenes with him, but the thought of him anywhere near her had me wanting to ring his fucking neck. The only reason why I didn't was because of my concern for Freya's health.

"We questioned the woman that left the bottle of water in her dressing room, but to be honest, I don't see her doing something like that, and there doesn't seem to be any motive." He inclines his head towards Freya as he continues. "Everyone says your woman keeps to herself. She doesn't stick around after work or party like most of them. The staff really like her, they say she is cordial and doesn't do tantrums like the other actors on set."

"She has a soft heart. I've seen that in her. I don't know how she got into the cutthroat career that she is in." I lift my hand, pulling my hair off my face.

"From what I've deduced, and from the information that Haldor has pulled up, there is only one person that would have anything to win from Freya's death." He takes a step towards me, glancing back at Freya as he says, "That person is Tanya Drafney. She is in debt, believe it or not, with all the money they make. Freya has been offered a part in a high-profile action movie that Tanya wants. I think that is motive enough to get rid of Freya."

I didn't know anything about this offer she got. Does she want to do it? Will I be able to stand around while she films all these scenes with different men? I know that if any of them touch her, there will be problems. They might as well just arrest me now and throw away the key, because I've just answered my own question. There is no way I can sit by and see some fucker kissing my woman, even if it's pretend.

"There is just one problem, Tanya Drafney is flying back home in another couple of days. If we want to get her for this, we need to act soon." All I want to do to her is place my hands around her throat and squeeze until I see her mean soul leave her body. If she had accomplished her goal, then Freya would have been dead by now. And I would soon follow because there is no way that an Elemental can live long after he has found the light—the goodness that is his woman. In the little time that I've had with Freya, I've realized that she is the pureness that is missing in me.

I'm darkness, rage, and revenge while she is my light, peace, and forgiveness. I know that without her I will continue in this world being angry at everyone and everything, never finding any peace or happiness. I knew that there was something missing from my life before I met my mate, but I didn't know to what extent. Now, after seeing the darkness that I am without Freya, there is no way that I can go back, and I will never allow myself to turn into a Keres.

"Does Tor know?" I've spent all my time with Freya, not leaving the room, therefore, I have no idea what they have been up to regarding the poisoning.

"No, I haven't spoken to him yet, but I will when I leave here. The problem is that the agent has reported it to the cops, so we are going to have to tell them what we know."

"Fuck, I swear that agent is a pain." I would love nothing more than to make that fucking woman pay for what she tried to do, but now I'm sure Tor will give the cops the information and let them take care of her.

"Also, we haven't let him up, but he has been here twice asking to see Freya."

"Fuck him. She doesn't need to deal with the likes of him while she's still not well, I mutter as I lean forward to stroke Frey's hair.

"You are going to have to let him see her soon or he might make a fuss." I know that what he is saying is true, but she has been through enough these last few days. I will have her get stronger before she needs to talk to anyone.

"When she's stronger, he can talk to her," I grumble, which has Asgar nodding before he turns to leave. Sitting here alone with Freya, I sigh, finally letting myself relax knowing that she is on her way to getting better. Flexing my neck, I try to relieve the tension there. It has been a couple of soul-wrenching days—days that I never want to go through again. I felt powerless sitting next to her hour after hour and not being able to help her. There was a stage where she was struggling to breathe. The overwhelming feeling of hopelessness that I felt at that moment is something that I've never felt before and something I never want to feel again.

Closing my eyes, I lean my head back against the headboard as I continue to stroke Freya's hair. I hear approaching footsteps, and sense Anastasia's energy as she nears. There is a light knock on the door before she opens it slowly. Opening my eyes, I see her peeping around the door.

"Hey, Dane."

Anastasia hasn't been with us long, but her presence has already been felt among us. Ulrich's woman has a way about her that makes me smile. She doesn't let Ulrich get away with much, but that is what he needs. Ulrich has always needed someone to ground him, and there is no one better than his mate.

"I thought I would sit with Freya so you can go shower, and then Monica will bring you some food." Anastasia has taken charge of the clubhouse after only a couple of months after being here, it is amusing to see how she gets the Jezebels to do her bidding. I remember her first decree to the Jezebels. She stated that Ulrich was off limits, and that if they didn't want all freezing hell breaking loose, they should listen. The funny part is that she probably meant it. She has a gift of ice and would probably freeze a poor woman just for touching Ulrich. I've noticed they have kept a wide berth around him now.

As Elementals, we don't care about any other woman but our mate once we bonded, so there would be no suspicion at all that Ulrich could step out on her. But if that made her feel more secure, she didn't show it, and we were just too entertained to tell her differently.

"It's fine, Anastasia, but thanks." She has been offering

to sit with Freya from the first day we brought her here, but not knowing if she could slip away while I was gone kept me vigilant at her side the whole time.

"Nonsense. Asgar just told us that Freya woke up, which means that she is getting better and will be fine in no time. Therefore, it's time for you to take care of yourself. So first, go shower. I'm sure you don't want her to relapse from the stink in here," she quips with a raised brow. "Then food because you're going to need your strength to sweet talk her into health, and after you eat, I think you need to sleep because I don't think you have slept much in these last few days." She isn't wrong. I've taken short naps while sitting next to Freya, but never fully went to sleep because I was worried that she would need me, and I wouldn't hear her.

"Has anyone told you that you should have been a sergeant?"

She grins. "I've learnt that being a sergeant is the only way to get you men to listen to me." She might be right where that is concerned. We pretty much do our own thing, not sticking to convention. I glance down at Freya to see she's peaceful, her colour is starting to improve, too. She was so pale before. "She will be fine while you shower, come on," she says, motioning her head towards the bathroom.

"Fine, bossy boots," I grumble, but I find it endearing that such a tiny little slip of a girl thinks she can bully men twice her size. Standing, I pull my t-shirt off. She gasps and I see her eyes widening. "What?"

"I'm sure you can get undressed in the bathroom," she whispers, which has me raise my eyebrows in question.

"I'm in my bedroom, last time I checked." My hands move to the button at the waistband of my jeans, which has her hurriedly turning around to face the door. I grin, I wasn't going to undress before her, but I wanted to show her that she won't be able to get everything her own way. Besides, Ulrich would have my hide if he knew I got undressed in front of his woman, like I would if they did it in front of Freya.

Turning, I head towards the bathroom. Slipping inside, I close the door behind me. I pull a clean towel from off the shelf and turn on the shower. Being next to my woman, even though she's been sick, has been hell on me. When she is one hundred percent recovered, I'm going to keep her in bed the whole day, taking her in every possible position known to me.

The warm water cascading over my body feels like heaven. My hand moves to my hardness. Just thinking about my woman has me hard and ready. I start stroking my length slowly at first, my eyes closed as I imagine myself kissing her perfect skin—caressing her silky thighs. Her perfect round breasts bobbing with her breathing. Her sweetness on my tongue as I kiss her heated core, hearing her gasps of pleasure.

My hand moves faster over my length. I feel my balls tightening as I feel myself reaching the pinnacle before I cum. My other hand snaps out flat against the tiles before me as I move my hand faster, tightening my hold just slightly as I feel the pressure build. I imagine Freya's mouth kissing my cock, taking it deep into her mouth. Fuck, I'm nearly there, squeezing my eyes tight as I stroke two more times before I'm grunting my release. Cum juts out against the shower wall, my cock spasming in my hand.

I know that this is a simple release. It can't compare to the release or pleasure I feel when I make love to Freya, but at least now I'm more relaxed and should be able to sleep without a hard-on from being next to my woman and not being able to touch her.

I let the water wash away all evidence of my cum, my muscles slowly relaxing as I wash with the shower gel. The smell of the natural herbs that are in the gel calm me. Some women in the Mother Chapter have opened a business where they produce natural products. Those products are mostly used by the Elementals, because I don't know what they use, but they are amazing. This shower gel, for example, really does relax the senses and the mind.

Turning off the tap, I step out of the shower, placing the towel around my hips as I walk into my bedroom to find Monica just about to leave from bringing my meal up. She stops when she sees me, turning she inclines her head towards the bed. "Anastasia says that she's your Ol' lady, is that true?" I've had quite a few good times with Monica, but that's all it ever was. Monica was never able to give me the absolute mind-blowing orgasms that Freya can or the complete feeling of peace that I feel when I'm near my woman.

"Yes, it is."

She nods then turns to leave. The women know not to try to entice us if we have an old lady, therefore, I know that Monica will keep her distance. The women were all sent away when Anastasia came to stay with us, but she felt guilty for having them leave their home, so she nagged Ulrich and Tor until they both gave in and brought them back, but only with the condition that if one of us has an old lady, then we are off bounds.

I know that the Jezebels respect Anastasia and I only hope that they will respect Freya too, because the last thing I need is problems with Freya because of them.

FREYA 10

It's a week after I was poisoned, and Dane is finally leaving me to my own devices for the first time. He's insisted on me staying in bed until I was strong enough, and even though I would never tell him, I've realized that he wouldn't let me leave the bed for a month if I had told him that I still feel a little weak, and that my head starts to spin whenever I sit up. But I'm glad to have a little time to myself just to process my thoughts and everything that has happened.

Dane left today because they are going to confront Tanya. The cops are aware of the interaction between them, as the Elementals are going to try to wiggle a confession out of her so that she can be arrested. Why,

why would she do this? I know that she has never liked me, but why destroy your life for greed? If she had only spoken to me, I would have told her that I wasn't going to take the new contract, but instead she decided to kill me. I shudder when I think of the last week and how lucky I am to be here.

Even though Dane has been overbearing and not wanting me to overdo things, he has been caring and always tries to keep me entertained. I lift my hand to my neck to feel the beautiful stone. When I woke up, I found this beautiful watermelon tourmaline around my neck. It is very similar to the one that Dane always wears, just smaller. Dane explained that when Elementals are born, two stones are chosen by their father. These stones are used in the naming ceremony. The stones are introduced to all the elements, and finally the energy of that baby is linked to the stone, which in turn, helps protect him and one day his mate.

Dane placed the stone around my neck when I was sick to try to protect and heal me. I know that for him and all the Elementals, their individual stones represent an important step in a relationship. Dane says that an Elemental giving their mate their stone is like getting married to a human. Therefore, I will honour him by always wearing it around my neck. This man that is my mate has many facets. I know that only with time, will I get to know all of them, but one that I've realized is that Dane is loyal and will do anything for those that are close to him.

Sliding to the side of the bed, I stand, closing my eyes as my head starts to spin. When it finally stops, I take a step, then another and another until I'm by the bedroom door. I'm sick and tired of being in this room, I'm dying to see the club. Yesterday I met Anastasia, and she seems nice, but only time will tell if she is what she seems, as I've come to realize throughout my life that people show one thing and then turn out to be completely different when it suits them.

I make my way down a corridor, hearing talking and music coming from the front. "I don't think you supposed to be out of bed, are you.?"

I gasp in fright, glancing behind me to see Tor. "Tor, you gave me a fright." He raises his brow and I feel that was his intention. "I'm fine, I was going crazy locked up in the room." He nods then motions his head towards where the noise is coming from.

"You sure you want to go into the bar area with all the noise and smoke in there?"

I sigh because that doesn't sound appealing at all.

"You can go into the kitchen, though, and get something to eat or coffee."

Now, that sounds much better.

Smiling at him, I nod. "Yes, I think coffee sounds perfect. Where is it?" Suddenly he grins, and I can't help myself but to stare. Tor is a big man, not as big as Dane, but close. His hair is a dark blond, long, and his unshaved stubble gives him a real Viking appearance. I'm not the only one that thinks so because the thin gold bands around his biceps tell me he also thinks highly of himself.

"Now, what kind of gentleman would I be if I didn't escort you there?"

At his comment, I want to laugh. Gentleman is the last thing I think anyone would ever call Tor.

He motions with his hand towards the end of the corridor which has me making my way there, feeling self-conscious of how slowly I'm walking as he follows right behind me. Entering the kitchen, I stop. There seems to be everything anyone could possibly need in this kitchen. It is clearly one of the most popular areas in the club, as the fridge is one of the biggest I've ever seen. There is a counter in the middle with a big fruit bowl in the centre. Cupboards run the length of the walls, which tells me that they are all full.

"Okay, take a seat," Tor says as he steps around me towards the kettle. "One coffee, coming up."

I pause. "Oh, you don't need to make me coffee." I never expected the president of Dane's charter to serve me.

"Nonsense, you're in no condition to be making your

own at the moment."

Well, one thing is clear; Dane takes after his leader with the protective streak. Tor brings me the coffee mug, placing it on the table. He then places the sugar bowl next to the coffee.

"Milk?"

"Yes, please."

After bringing the milk and placing it before me, he takes a seat opposite me, which makes me uncomfortable. Tor is a formidable presence. Even though he is friendly, he also has a dangerous essence around him.

"What are you planning to do with your filming career?"

Well, talk about coming straight to the point.

"What do you mean?"

"I mean that your profession will have you flying all around the world. Being an Elemental's mate doesn't allow for you to be away from your mate for long. You'll physically start to waste away without each other. So how do you see it going?" I hadn't really thought about it to be fair. I had already decided I wasn't going to sign the contract for the next movie, but I hadn't thought about my future.

Shrugging, I take a sip of my coffee before answering. "I

have a contract with my agent, which I need to adhere to, but besides that I haven't committed to anything else. I was going to take a break before making any more movies."

Tor nods at my answer. "You are now part of the family; the Elementals stick together no matter what. Even though we argue, we all care for each other and would die before letting harm come to another. If you have a problem, and Dane isn't around, you can talk to any of us and we'll help." I've never had much of a family before, except my mom, and she's not around much. This is going to be strange for me, but I'm pleased to know that he accepts me.

"So, this is where you got to?" I glance towards the kitchen door to see a smiling Anastasia. I really hope she's as nice as she seems.

"She needed Caffeine," Tor quips, winking at me as he stands to make his way towards the door.

"Thank you, Tor."

Tor doesn't slow down, but he does lift his hand in acknowledgment

"So, how are you feeling today?" Anastasia asks as she sits in Tor's chair.

"I'm feeling better, but try tell Dane that," I say with a shrug. "I just needed to get out of the room. I was also curious to see the club."

"Oh, great!" Anastasia says, clapping her hands in excitement. "I will introduce you to everyone you haven't met." I place my empty mug on the counter as I stand slowly, so I don't get dizzy.

"I'm ready," I say with a smile. My head is still slightly woozy, which has me holding onto the counter.

"Are you sure, sweetheart?" Anastasia asks as she places her hand on my back.

"Yes. I just get dizzy when I stand, but then I'm fine." I smile at her. "So, where are we going?"

"Well, let me show you the club, but we will skip the bar area. There are members from another club visiting at the moment, and the men get really touchy when they start looking at me, and now you, too, I'm guessing."

"Dane is really possessive. Are you telling me they all are?"

"Well, let's just say it is part of their DNA, and because you are with an Elemental, you are off bounds." I'm so tired of having people always ogling me, wanting to know everything about my life that the thought of no one being able to talk or look at me, pleases me in a weird way.

"I'm leaving now." My eyes snap to the man by the door looking at the two of us. His cocky smile screams naughtiness. I have no doubt in my mind that this one is always getting himself into trouble.

"Oh, wait. Let me introduce you to Dane's mate."

He nods at me, but his eyes return to Anastasia. "How about kissing me goodbye?" His raised brow has a boyish quality that makes me smile. So, this must be Anastasia's mate. I think she called him Ulrich.

"Not if you are going to be rude," she says as she raises her chin.

One minute Ulrich is by the door, the next his hands are on Anastasia's hips, his lips all over hers. I smile when I see her hands snaking up around his shoulders. Well, it looks like these two will be interesting to watch, and one thing I love to do is watch people.

When Ulrich finally raises his head, I can see a dazed smile on Anastasia's face. If Ulrich kisses anything like Dane, then I understand that smile. Every time Dane touches me, I forget everything and everyone around me and only he matters.

"Be good," he grunts as he slaps her ass gently before turning to leave. "Nice meeting you, Star," he finally says without another glance at me. I'm guessing the name Star is for me being an actress.

"Likewise," I call after him as I glance at Anastasia to see her still looking after her man. "Well, I'm guessing I've just met Ulrich, unless you were kissing someone else?"

At my cheeky comment, I see her cheeks redden with colour. "Oh, I'm sorry about that," she says as she raises her hand to her cheek. "He's so hot, isn't he? Not, that I would ever say that in front of him. His ego is way too big already."

She makes me grin at the disgruntled statement. "I might be wrong, but all the men I've met seem to have a sickeningly high sex appeal. That is very hard to find in such abundance."

My comment has her laughing. She nods as she places her arm through mine. "You are so right, but you know what I've come to realize?"

I shake my head as she doesn't seem to continue until I answer.

"They have the softest hearts. Any one of them would go out of their way to help another."

"Do they all know that you have an ice gift?" I'm still unsure of how much to trust everyone around me. Anastasia told me about her gift, but it was hard for me to believe her.

"Of course, after all, they aren't exactly plain. If you know what I mean?"

I still can't believe half the things that I've learnt since I met Dane, but I feel like deep down, I've known there was something more to this world all along.

"Now, let me show you the best place at the club." Anastasia guides me down the corridor and to the right. Opening a door, she stands back for me to enter. Walking in, I stop, stunned.

"Wow!" I can't believe what they have in here. There is a swimming pool that looks more like something you would get on a set for the movie *Arabian Nights*. I can spy what looks like a sauna in one corner, and then in the far corner is a door that looks like it leads into a training room.

"Impressive, isn't it?"

I like swimming, but it isn't exactly my type of thing. I'm not an exercising type of person, and I'm more of the sitting somewhere cosy with a book kind of girl.

"There is even a sun bed, which no one uses. You will find that Tor likes to have all the latest gadgets." Anastasia points towards the door that I assume holds a training room. "That there is the training room, and besides the kitchen and bar, one of the most used rooms in the club."

We make our way there, entering I see a man in the far corner punching a boxing bag. Again, there is everything a person could need in this room. "Have you met Einar?" I shake my head as I see the man stop his training to turn to us. Wow, Einar has the lightest green eyes I've ever seen. His dark, straight, black hair is a contrast that keeps your eyes on him. The man is stunning, but there is an animalistic aura around him that makes you weary.

"Einar, this is Dane's mate Freya." The way his eyes catch and hold mine feels like he is reading my very soul. This man is intense.

"You seem better." His voice is hypnotic like his eyes, everything about this man cries danger.

"I am," I reply with a tentative smile, but he doesn't smile back, just continues looking at me.

"We will see you later, Einar." Anastasia says as she turns, placing her arm through mine to guide me out of the training room and pool area. Once we are outside in the corridor again, she stops. "Don't mind, Einar. He doesn't talk much, but he's a great guy."

"Yes, looks very friendly."

At my sarcastic comment, she bursts out laughing. "All the guys here are intense in one way or another. You will get used to it, and you will end up loving them, trust me."

I don't know so much about loving or trusting them, but I'm willing to give them a chance. Anastasia walks towards a door which opens to the outside. Stepping out, I smile. *Now this is more like it.*

"I see that you like this," Anastasia states, noticing my smile of pleasure

"I love nature, and this is absolutely beautiful." I look around at the beautiful enclosed landscaped garden. It looks like Tor really does like his creature comforts. "I could spend my life sitting here," I murmur as I see various types of birds eating from a bird feeder that has been set near a little brook of water.

"You would never say this was here, would you?"

I shake my head. "There's a man here to see you." My head snaps around to see a woman standing by the door. "He says he's your agent." She doesn't wait for a reply as she turns to leave.

"And that was Tracy. Don't mind her, she's always like that with new people."

"Whose mate, is she?"

I see Anastasia lift a brow and then grin. "Well, now, that is a long story." And with those words she inclines her head towards the door. "Shall we go?" I frown but nod. The last thing I feel like doing right now is talking to Tom, but I guess I need to do it sooner or later.

"I still want to hear that long story," I say, which has Anastasia laughing.

"I'm sure you do."

DANE 11

We left home early to catch Tanya Drafney still in her hotel. The cops will be listening in on our questioning of her because the fucking agent told them we suspected Tanya and were going to speak to her. Tor thought it better to play along with them. I personally would rather make her pay for what she did, but now that I have a mate, I need to think of all the consequences of my actions. We need to get Tanya to confess to the poisoning accusation because it's the only way this will work.

"Are you ready?" Haldor asks as we step out of the lift. The receptionist was not happy to see us again, but Tal is downstairs with him to appease his fears, and make sure he doesn't call security on us until we are ready. Having the cops with us also helped, which had him looking at us suspiciously.

"Yeah, just want to get this over and done with." Stepping up to Tanya's hotel room door, Haldor knocks, I can hear her mumbling inside as she steps towards the door. "Showtime," I mutter as she opens the door, gasping when she sees us.

"What do you want?" Her voice is irritating, I would like nothing more than to shut her up.

"We need to ask you some questions," Haldor states, as he leans against the doorframe.

"Well, I'm busy, and you shouldn't be here. I'm going to complain to the management of this hotel on the type of people they let in here."

"You're right, their guests have much to be desired," I quip sarcastically at the stupid bitch's comment.

She gasps, glaring at me. "Leave, or I will call security."

"Sure, go ahead. We'll share with them the information we have on you," Haldor says with a shrug which has her turning to him in shock, her eyes suspicious.

"There is nothing you can have on me," she challenges, refusing to move from the doorway.

"Except evidence that you poisoned Freya."

She tenses at the accusation and now there is fear in her eyes, which is more like the reaction I was expecting.

"Nonsense, you can't have any evidence." But there is uncertainty in her voice and her head turns so she can look up and down the corridor to make sure we are alone.

"Okay then, we will just take what we have to the cops and see what they think of it," I inform her, turning as if I'm about to leave.

"Wait..." Her panic is evident now. "What do you want?"

"How much is our silence worth to you?" Haldor asks

"How do I know you're not bluffing?"

"Look, we all know you are responsible for poisoning Freya. You were sloppy and left evidence all over the place."

"I was not sloppy! I wore gloves, and no one saw me."

Well, there is her confession; that is all we needed. "All of that for money?" I growl, disgusted with her coldness. "You nearly killed a woman."

She shakes her head in anger. "I'm just sorry she didn't

die."

I snap, my once tight control unravels like a ball of wayward yarn. I lift my hand up, snatching her around the neck before I push her body hard against the wall.

"What?" she gasps.

"Dane," Haldor warns as he places his hand around my bicep and pulls. "Let her go, Brother." I would rather twist her scrawny neck, but I can hear the cops rushing towards us, so I reluctantly let go.

"You will get everything you deserve," I say softly near her ear just as the cops reach us.

"Oh… thank goodness you're here," she gasps, pointing at me. "These men attacked me."

"Tanya Drafney, you are under arrest for attempted murder." I step back, letting the cop near her so he can cuff her. "Anything you say, can and will be held against you in a court of law."

I turn, making my way back towards the lift. Haldor is speaking to one of the cops, but I'm tired of all this and just want to get back. I make my way out of the hotel towards the bikes.

"How did it go?" Tal asks when I sit on my bike waiting for Haldor to join us.

"We got her."

This has Tal slapping his handlebars in pleasure. "Great, one threat down," he says with a grin. "Another lurking."

His cryptic statement has me raising my eyes to his. "What?" I ask.

"The Desperados are tagging us."

I grunt as I surreptitiously look around, noticing a van parked up the road. Two of the Desperados members are sitting inside. Dag and I were looking for the woman Esmeralda the day Freya was poisoned. We had three of their men approach us to threaten that if we didn't leave the search of the woman to them, then we might find ourselves dead. Since then, I haven't asked what has been happening with the search for Esmeralda, but whatever it is, it has them following us.

"Dag still trying to find her?" I ask.

"Yeah, he seems obsessed," Tal confirms.

"I'm going to go and ask them what they want," I say, bored to be sitting here waiting for Haldor.

"Wait for me," Tal says as he follows me. When we get a couple of cars before them, the driver starts the van, and then he is revving his engine just before he pulls down the road. "Looks like they don't want to talk, just watch."

I don't like knowing that I have eyes on me. If I see one

of those fuckers again, I will show them how much I don't like it.

"We better tell Dag," I grumble.

"Do you think this Esmeralda is his mate?" Tal asks as we make our way back to our bikes.

"Yeah, he is way to obsessed with finding this woman for her not to be his mate."

"Fuck, you guys are falling like flies," Tal grunts with a frown.

Our conversation comes to an end when Haldor approaches. "A good day's work. Shall we go relax?" he asks with a wink as he lifts his helmet from his handlebars before swinging his leg over the bike. The three of us take off down the road towards the club, heading home to my woman. I wonder if she's still relaxing in bed like I told her, or if she got tired of sitting and went looking around?

Before leaving, I asked Tor to have someone keep an eye on her just in case she did decide to not listen to me and go exploring. Even though she doesn't admit to it, she's still weak, and can fall easily and hurt herself. We pull up to the club. I can already hear the music and loud voices from inside. Looking at the bikes that are parked outside, I would say that some of the members of the Skulls MC decided to pay us a visit.

The Skulls dabble in contraband and drugs, but they are small-fry compared to some of the other MC clubs in the area.

"Hey, about time you joined us," Trigger calls from one of the tables. Camille is sitting on his lap, stroking his neck. "I was thinking that we had to have this party by ourselves." Trigger is the Skulls enforcer, and a loudmouth most of the time. I see that Blade, Tiny, and Jughead are also here.

Tor is absent, but Garth and Asger are sitting with the men. "Don't tell me you were missing us?" Haldor laughs as he approaches them.

"Your ugly mug? Never," Tiny quips as he slaps Tracy's ass just as she bends down to place fresh bottles of beer on the table.

"Dane," Blade calls as I lean over the bar to grab a bottle of water. "I hear you got yourself an old lady."

I still, glancing back at him. "And where would you hear that?" I ask. The only people that know about Freya being my old lady are the men in the club and I doubt they would say anything.

"Let's just say, a little bird told me," Blade says with a wink at Tracy, which tells me she's the one that told them.

"When are you getting one, or do the women all run

away from your romantic charms?" Tal interrupts with a grin that has Blade chuckle.

"They love my romantic charms. What are you talking about?" I walk towards the corridor; I want to see how Freya is doing before I have to entertain the Skulls. I turn towards where the rooms are located but sense that Freya is in the kitchen. Shaking my head, I grin, realizing that she must have got tired of sitting in the room by herself. Approaching, I stop when I hear her agent's voice. The fucker finds a gap, and he is here like the fucking flash.

I swear if he upsets her, I will ring his fucking neck. Stepping into the kitchen, I see Freya sitting on one of the chairs, Anastasia next to her. Both are looking at the agent that is pacing before them.

"You shouldn't be out of bed," I say, which has the Agent stopping to look at me.

Freya rolls her eyes in irritation at my words, which would have me grinning if it wasn't for her fucking agent being here.

"I'm fine. Besides, I'm sitting down, just not in bed."

"Can we get back to the issue at hand here?" her agent interrupts angrily.

"I don't see an issue, Tom; you just say no to them," Freya answers sweetly, but I can tell that she's irritated.

"You don't see an issue? Don't see an issue?" his petulant, overbearing tone is starting to irritate me. "You can't just pull away from over a million dollar contract."

"Why not?" Anastasia asks. "She hasn't signed anything."

What the fuck is this about?

"Keep out of this, young lady." His condescending tone at Anastasia has me stepping towards him.

"Listen here, you fucker." I raise my hands to grip his shirt.

"Freeze," Freya says in an angry tone. I know she doesn't want problems, but this son of a bitch needs to understand that he doesn't talk to women like that. Taking hold of his shirt, I shake him, but to my surprise he is as stiff as a board and he doesn't say anything. Looking at his face, I see that his eyes are open, his mouth too, as if he was about to say something, but he is frozen in place.

"Why aren't you two frozen?" Freya asks with a frown.

I turn my head to look at her and see that she is looking at Anastasia and me in surprise. "Were you trying to freeze me?" *She wouldn't dare, would she?*

"Yes, I didn't feel like having to appease Tom just so you don't go to jail. Now do you mind leaving him alone?" I look back at the asshole and drop my hands.

"Wow, that's so cool," Anastasia says as she stands to hurry around the table to look at the agent. "How long will it last?" she asks.

Freya shrugs. "Until I tell it to stop, or after an hour or so."

"Why didn't it work with you two?" she questions, still frowning.

"Your gifts don't work on Elementals. Anastasia has our blood, so it won't work on her either," I state, approaching her cautiously.

"Great," she groans sarcastically.

"What the fuck is he complaining about?" I ask.

"There is a new movie that he wants Freya to star in. She gave him his contract back but didn't sign it, telling him that she's not interested. You came in just in time to hear him telling her that he doesn't think it's a good idea," Anastasia says as she goes to sit back down next to Freya.

"You don't want to do this movie?" I didn't know anything about this contract. I don't want Freya to stop doing something just because of us. The last thing I want is for my woman to resent our bond because of her career.

"No. I already told him that."

The weight that was starting to build on my shoulders disburses. "Well then, I will make him understand," I say as I turn back to the asshole.

"No, Dane." I look back at her and see the determination in her eyes. "I want to do this myself, please."

Fuck, how can I refuse that? "Fine, but if he…"

Freya interrupts by saying, "I need you to leave so I can do this myself, because I know that you'll interrupt."

I tense, leaving her here with a man that I know is arguing with her goes against everything I stand for. "No, I won't touch him, but if need be, I will tell him to get the fuck out." She must take it or leave it. There's no way I'm leaving my woman with this man to be verbally abused.

"Fine, but please let me try to resolve this first."

I nod.

"Now, go stand where you were before."

I frown at her bossy tone before doing her bidding.

"Unfreeze." The minute Freya says the word, her agent lifts his hands in the air as if warding off an attack, then he frowns when he sees us all looking at him. Wow, my woman has a cool gift even if she did want to use it on me.

I manage to keep out of the argument except to tell the fucker to watch his words when he raises his voice. But besides that, it went well. My woman held firm to her decision, and he had to concede in defeat, leaving in anger.

FREYA 12

Now that Tanya has been locked up, and Tom has conceded to my wishes, I'm happy. I've now met everyone in the club and even though I'm still weary of some of them, I'm starting to relax more and take it one day at a time. Dane is amazing. He has managed to sweep me off my feet every chance he gets. It has been two weeks since the day Dane conceded to let me fight my own battle with Tom, and since then, he has tried to be more understanding of my needs.

Dane is an alpha male through and through, I doubt anything will change that, but the fact that he goes against his basic instincts to please me, tells me more than most things. He also has a romantic side to him that surprised me. Two days ago, I entered the room to find candles littered all around the room, petals on the ground, and a blanket with a picnic basket on the ground near one of the windows.

Then this morning, he came to our room, grabbed my hand, and started guiding me outside without saying anything, no matter how much I asked. He wanted to show me a patch of land behind the garden that he cordoned off for me to plant my herbs and flowers. In these last two weeks, we have both gotten to know each other quite well. We stay up sometimes until the early hours of the morning, talking about our likes, dislikes, and things that have happened in our lives.

I know Dane will frustrate me sometimes with his quick temper and protective streak, but I also know that he will make me happy, because Dane is everything I could ever want in a man. From the minute I met him, I knew that what we have together was special and I could trust him, but I didn't know that we would fit so well together.

"Are you ready?" I turn to see him standing in the bedroom doorway. He asked if I would like to go for a ride today, and because I've secretly been hoping for another chance on the back of his bike, I immediately said yes.

"Yes." I make my way to him as he holds up a kutte.

"This is for you." He turns the kutte around and I see that it has the Elemental's logo in the middle of the back with "Property of Dane" below it. Anastasia told me that when there is a party in the club that it is important to always wear our kutte because that will tell everyone that we are taken.

"Does this make it official? Am I your old lady now?" I ask with a smile as he helps me put on the kutte.

"You have been my old lady from the minute I saw you in that garden, so it's not a kutte that's going to do that." He lowers his head, kissing my neck, which has me leaning my head back against his shoulder. Dane's kisses are like ambrosia, I've never tasted anything better in my life. Every time he touches me it's like the first time, there is an excitement there that leaves me wanting more.

I'm like a teenager with her first crush, I think about Dane all the time and when he's close, I don't want to let him out of my sight. "We better go, Ulrich and Anastasia are coming with us."

I smile. Anastasia hasn't let me down yet. I know that I've been weary and always hold people at arm's length, but she seems to be genuine, and I'm starting to realize that everyone here is exactly as they seem, and it's all starting to feel very real.

"Where are we going?"

"The mountain passes in Cape Town are great to ride, so I thought we would take that route, stopping for lunch near the ocean, so you can wet your feet if you like."

I laugh. That is the only thing I would ever dip into the ocean. The waters around here are freezing cold.

"Do you think we might see some whales?" He takes my hand, guiding me down the corridor to the bar area.

"At this time of year, you might." I've always wanted to see the whales, and now I might get the chance. I'm so excited that when I walk into the bar area, I don't realize the deathly quiet until Dane stops and I feel him stilling next to me.

"What's wr. . ."

"Freya..."

Hearing my mom's voice makes me pause. My head snaps around to see her standing next to Tom. *What the hell game is he playing by bringing my mom here?*

"Mom, what are you doing here?" My mother has never left Missouri, so for her to be here in South Africa, Tom must have gone to fetch her and promised her something substantial.

"Mom?" Dane asks, looking down at me. I squeeze his

hand gently because I've told him about my strained relationship with my mother.

"Can't I come and see my own daughter?"

I nod, letting go of Dane's hand so I can walk towards her. We haven't been around each other in such a long time that this feels awkward. I hug her and feel her stiffen in response. *Well, I guess that hasn't changed.*

"Where are you staying?" I ask.

"Tom has kindly booked a room for me at the Quartz Hotel." Something is up. Tom doesn't do anything without a motive, and he doesn't spend his money unless he's getting something out of it.

"Why didn't you tell me you were coming?" I see my mom glance behind me and know that she's looking at Dane. "Mom, I would like you to meet Dane." Glancing over my shoulder, I see him standing with his arms crossed looking at us.

At my introduction, he nods his head but doesn't say anything, which works because my mom completely ignores his greeting.

"Can we talk somewhere in private?"

And here it comes. I nod, then make my way towards the corner table. I see that Tom accompanies us, which tells me that this is definitely his doing. I know that wherever Dane is in the room, he will hear our conversation clearly, so no matter where we sit, he will still hear what they have to say.

When we are all sitting, I wait for my mom to say why she is here. I don't have to wait long, because she leans forward. "What do you think you are doing?"

I raise a brow. *What is she talking about?*

She motions with her hand to the bar and Dane. "You are better than this," she whispers.

"Are you telling me that you came all this way to tell me that I have a bad taste in men?"

"Are you on drugs?"

"What?" *How can she ask me that?* She hasn't been in my life for years, and now out of the blue she's acting concerned?

"Well, everything else doesn't make sense, so you must be on drugs," she snaps.

"Actually no, I'm not on drugs and have never done drugs in my life," I mutter angrily. "Not that you would know anything about that."

"This doesn't make sense." She motions again to the bar. "You come to live here when you can live anywhere you want in the world, and you turn down an opportunity of a lifetime. Are you crazy?"

"This is really underhanded, even for you, Tom," I argue, knowing what his angle is now by bringing my mom here. He must have thought that me seeing her would change my mind about signing the contract. Well, he was very wrong. If anything, it has shown me the difference between the life I had and the life I have now.

"I'm your agent; it is my responsibility to make sure that you make the right decisions." I would fire him, but I know that he would sue me for breach of contract, and I would have to pay him a fortune, so I don't.

"I'm the one that decides on my life, and this is what I want."

"What is that?" my mom asks as she looks around. "What can you possibly want here, when you can have anything you want?"

"Mom, you don't know this, but I wasn't happy. This, the people that live here, all of it makes me happy." I shake my head, sad that I need to have this conversation with my own mother. "They understand me, and they care about me, something that I didn't find with anyone else."

"Don't be blind. All they want is your money."

"The only person I give money to is you, Mom, no one else. So, it seems like the only person that is interested in my money is you."

I can see her face flush in anger, I don't remember her being so hungry for money when I was younger or so self-conscious of her appearance. Her manicured nails and dyed hair, professes that she is careful in caring for herself. Is that what she is worried about, that the money will stop going to her?

"Nonsense, I'm your mother. I have a right to your money, these people don't!"

Is she serious? Does she really think that just because she birthed me that she has a right to my assets?

"Look, I'm sorry you had to come all this way, but I'm not changing my mind. This is now my home and what I do with my life has nothing to do with either of you."

"Stop being stubborn Freya, you are ruining your career by not accepting this contract," she fires angrily.

"No, Mom, I fixed my life by not accepting the contract. Now, if you two will excuse me, we were just on our way out. I'm sorry, Mom, that you had to come all this way, but you should have phoned." Standing, I turn to make my way towards Dane, but stop when my mother takes my hand.

"Don't do this, Freya. I will contest this and tell the judge that you're not in your right mind."

Can she do that? I turn to face her, my anger now as palpable as hers.

"You do that. Good luck in trying to prove it." I pull my hand away and make my way towards Dane. An overwhelming feeling of sorrow fills me that my mother wants to take me to court, all because she doesn't agree with my decisions.

"You know I can tell them you are unstable. You know I can," she threatens.

Looking up at Dane, I see his furious expression. I know that he didn't interrupt our conversation because I want to resolve my own problems, but by his white knuckles, I can tell he would have loved nothing more than to have thrown both of them out of here.

"Can we please go," I whisper.

He nods, slipping his arm around my shoulders as he guides us out. I hear my mother say something else and then Tom answer, but the minute Dane places his arm around me it feels like everything around me stilled.

"When we get outside, Ulrich and Anastasia are already sitting on his bike. Dag is leaning against his, which gives me the impression that he's also accompanying us. Eirik walks towards us from the workshop with his helmet in hand.

"Everything okay?" Dag asks with a raised brow as he inclines his head towards the bar. Looking over my shoulder, I see my Mom standing by the door with one of her hands on her hip.

"It is now," I murmur, taking my helmet from Dane's hand and slipping it on.

"Okay then, let's do this," Ulrich says as he starts his bike and pulls away.

When we are all on the road, Dane squeezes my knee gently. "You okay?" I tighten my arms around his midriff and nod.

"Yes." I still feel a sorrow deep in my soul, knowing that my own mother would threaten to expose me all because of greed. What is the matter with people? Is money the only thing that makes them happy? That is why being with the Elementals feels so right. I don't see greed in any of them, and they genuinely care about each other.

My mother said that I must be crazy, and that I'm messing up my life. Well, the only thing that I'm sorry about is that I didn't pull away from that life before now—a life of constant betrayal and conspiracy of being among traitorous people. I'd like to know that the people I'm dealing with are not trying to betray me. That lifestyle was sucking my very soul dry, and she thinks I made a mistake?

Only now that I'm among the Elementals, do I realize how very sad I was. How depressed I was in all the coldness that surrounded me. I'm a giving person. I thrive in helping others, but when I realized that they were only with me because of what they could gain, it killed all the joy I got in helping them.

"Thank you," I murmur.

"For what?" I hear him ask.

"For finding me."

DANE 13

Her words are still playing in my mind as we ride through the twisting roads. This was supposed to be the perfect day. The weather is perfect, and Freya is finally back to her full strength. But then her mother showed up and threw a wrench in everything. How can a mother be like that?

I will make sure that my woman is as happy as she can possibly be. She has been rejected for long enough when her only crime is being too good to people. I will always protect her and her heart. From now on, I will tell the prospects that no one is allowed in to see Freya unless I tell them it's okay. I will not have any more surprises like that again.

If her mom thinks that she's going to get Freya's hard-earned money, then she doesn't know who she is dealing with. As Elementals, we have made a lot of connections throughout the years, and I will make sure that those connections give us all the help we need if her threat goes forward.

It's unbelievable that a mother who has been absent for most of her child's life, now feels it's her right to take her money. I blame that asshole agent for getting her mother involved and bringing her here. I think it's time to go pay him a visit and reason with him.

For now, I'm going to try to get Freya's mind off them and give her the best day possible. Ulrich is ahead of us. We discussed what route to take earlier, so I know that we are headed towards a little restaurant by the ocean. That will give the women a chance to go down to the water if they want, because the restaurant is a couple of steps away from the beach.

We slow our bikes as we near the little town where the restaurant is situated. The beautiful white houses with their blue painted doors and windowsills create a breath-taking picture. I look in my rear-view mirror to see Dag and Eirik following behind us. After Freya's recovery, I went to Eirik and apologized for my accusations. He wasn't upset, but I still felt like shit because I know that he protected her as well as anyone else would.

My quick temper has me reacting sometimes before I think, and I find that when it comes to Freya, my protective instinct has me more volatile when she's in danger. Parking the bike in front of the restaurant, I help Freya off. "Are you enjoying the ride so far?"

She smiles, handing me her helmet. "I love it, I don't know how I've gone twenty-five years without knowing what it felt like to be on a motorcycle."

"We should both learn how to ride, then we can have our own motorcycles," Anastasia says in excitement as she walks towards us. Ulrich has his arm around her shoulders, but he suddenly drops it and stops. I understand his reaction because no matter how I like the idea of Freya riding next to me, I love having her sit behind me, her arms around my waist. Besides, it's too dangerous for them to ride on their own.

"No."

I see Anastasia's body go rigid as she snaps around to look at Ulrich.

"What do you mean no?" Ulrich never thinks before he talks, he should have approached this topic in a different way. His aversion to the idea is just going to be an incentive for Anastasia to rebel and learn how to ride. If she wants to do it, then I'm sure Freya will be happy to learn as well, by the way she is taking to being on a motorcycle.

"It's too dangerous for you."

Oh man, I should just interrupt him now.

"Too dangerous for me, but not too dangerous for you?" Her hands are on her hips now and she doesn't seem pleased.

"Don't be upset. It's not you. It's the other fuckers on the road," he says as he throws his hands up in the air. "I like having you ride with me." Now he's starting to think, but it might be too late.

Anastasia huffs in irritation as she turns towards us again.

"I actually think it's a good idea," Freya pipes in.

Fuck, I knew it. "I like feeling you behind me, but if you want to learn I will teach you," I grunt, glaring at Ulrich. If he had kept his mouth shut, this would have gone differently.

"Now, why couldn't you say something like that?" Anastasia challenges.

"What do you mean? I did. I told you I like having you ride with me," he says in exasperation, which has Anastasia shaking her head and sighing as she steps away from him to draw her arm through Freya's.

"Shall we go down to the water while these cavemen find a table?" Great, now she's taking Freya with her.

"You really don't think before you speak, do you?" I groan to Ulrich when the women are a couple of steps ahead.

"What, are you saying that you're okay with your woman riding?" he asks with a raised brow.

"No, but you don't tell them they can't do it. You need to convince them that it's a bad idea. What would you do if someone told you not to do something?"

Ulrich shrugs with a scowl on his face. "I would go and do it."

"Exactly, so why would you think that they are different?"

"Did Ulrich stick his foot in it again?" Dag asks as he and Eirik come to stand next to us.

"No, he stuck both of them in deep, and now I will probably have to teach Freya how to ride because of him." I don't mind teaching her how to ride. What I do mind is if she decides that she wants her own motorcycle. "Someone teach him some finesse," I glare as I snap around and start making my way towards the restaurant.

"Look who's talking," Ulrich grunts as he follows me.

"Are you sure you want to find your mate?" I hear Eirik ask.

Glancing back, I see Dag nod, a frown replacing the smile on his face. "You have no idea how much it drives me. I just saw her on a photo, but it's engraved in my mind, and all I can think about is that she's in trouble and at any moment, she could get caught and Sean might kill her.

"I don't think he will catch her that easily. It looks like your woman is resourceful," I assure him as we continue walking. "She has been on the run for going on three weeks now, and even though he has everyone out looking for her, no one has found any sign of her."

"Fuck, I just wish I knew where she was," Dag says with a shake of his head.

"Why don't you ask Draco's woman, Katrina? You know she can find people and things," Ulrich suggests as we walk into the restaurant.

"Motherfucker, why the hell didn't I think of that?" Dag immediately pulls out his phone. "I'll be right in." He walks back outside to dial Draco. I hope he does find his mate because after finding Freya, I've found a calmness in myself that I never thought possible. The restaurant has windows all around, which allows for us to look towards the water where the women are standing.

"Let's sit outside on the balcony," Ulrich says as he starts making his way there, not waiting for the waiter to come and sit us. I see the waiter hesitate when he meets my eye, I point outside to the balcony where

Ulrich is now pulling out a chair and not waiting for his approval. Pulling back a chair, I face the water so I can always see Freya. She must have felt my eyes on her because she glances back, raising her hand to wave.

"How is she taking being mated to you?"

I raise my brows at Eirik's question. "Well, I am a really good catch."

At my quip, both Eirik and Ulrich start grinning.

"You keep lying to yourself like that, and soon you will start believing it," Ulrich teases.

I throw him the finger.

"Who's lying to themselves?" Dag asks as he takes a seat to my left.

"Dane," Eirik answers. "He says he's a very good catch."

Dag chuckles. It seems like the call has given him some peace about finding his mate. "Like a beached whale," he laughs. "Unmovable, big, and hard work." Dag's joke has all of us laughing.

"Good Afternoon, I will be your waitress for the day." The waitress, a girl that must be about eighteen, says smiling widely at all of us.

"Well hello, darling, you have just brightened our day," Eirik says, which has me grinning.

The girl flushes in embarrassment. "Umm, here are your menus. I'll be back in a minute to take your order," she says hurriedly as she places the menus on the middle of the table and scurries away.

"You frightened the poor girl with your ugly mug," Ulrich teases.

"No, I think it was his sad attempt at flirting."

Eirik grins before winking. "You guys are all just jealous because I'm the only one at the table that actually can flirt with anyone I want." That is true, except for the jealous part. Looking up once again at Freya, I see her and Anastasia making their way up towards us, a smile on both of their faces. I'm not jealous of not having the desire to flirt with another woman. Throughout my three hundred and twenty years, I've flirted and bedded lots of women, and never in all those years have I felt the way I feel now when I look at Freya.

"Have the drinks been ordered yet?" Anastasia asks as the women join us. Freya takes the seat to my right; a contented smile is on her face. I've realized that my woman is at her happiest among nature. Placing my arm behind her chair, I pull her closer. I hear her gasp in surprise, but then she relaxes and leans back.

"Not yet, Eirik frightened the waitress away," Ulrich replies.

Eirik grunts just as the waitress returns.

"What did you do? Don't tell me you embarrassed the poor thing." Anastasia asks with a smile as she looks at the waitress returning to our table.

"Are you ready to order?" she asks, but I notice she keeps her eyes away from Eirik, her cheeks warming with colour. The poor kid is innocent, and knowing Eirik, I know that he would never consider anything with someone so young.

The rest of the meal continues with the same light spirits until we finally get up to leave after eating. I know that Freya hasn't had many friendships, and usually keeps to herself, but I want her to get to know everyone, and realize that no one in the club would ever hurt her or betray her trust. We stick together— our word is our bond.

Starting the bikes, we once again make our way towards the club. We are a couple of miles away when suddenly my senses tell me that something is wrong. As we go around a bend, I see a van across the road. There is no way we are getting across. Slowing the bikes, we come to a stop.

"Something is fucking wrong," I growl, but know the others feel it, too.

"There is no one in the van," Dag states, just as the first shot is heard. I'm off the bike and have Freya on the ground under me before a second one can be fired.

"Fuck me," Dag mutters as the smell of blood hits me. Glancing over at him I see him lying on his back on the ground.

"Motherfuckers," I roar as another shot whizzes past my head.

"They're up on the ridge," Eirik points out.

"Ulrich, cloak Dag." Being shot, he's more vulnerable than the rest of us. When Ulrich and Anastasia bonded, we found that With Ulrich being able to bend fire and Anastasia able to freeze anything, she combines their powers together in her mind, so she can create enough of a fog to cloak us when we need it. We have never used it in a real situation, but we sure will use it now.

We hear another shot and then Freya screams "Freeze!"

Looking up, I see the fucking bullet frozen in the air a couple of feet away from Eirik's head.

"Shit," he mutters when he sees it, too.

"They're still up there," Ulrich grunts as the fog starts to rise, I see him wielding fire in a line on the ground and Anastasia has frozen the solid area around it which builds up condensation.

"My voice doesn't reach up there," I hear Freya say in frustration, which gives me an idea.

"When I say now, you scream it again, okay?"

I feel her nod below me, turning slightly so that my hands are free. I start manipulating the air around us, and then I'm pushing it up towards the men on the top of the ridge.

"Now," I say near her ear as the wind whistles with its full strength.

"Freeze!" she shouts, which has the wind pushing it up and towards the men.

"It worked," Eirik says as he stands. "I can see the two fuckers just standing there like statues." He then looks at Freya and winks. "I think I want you with us every time we ride."

"Dag, how are you, Brother?" I ask as I help Freya sit up but manoeuvre her behind my motorcycle just in case they come out of their statue state before we get to them.

"Fucking shot," he groans.

"Are you dying?" I know he isn't by his mutterings.

"Very funny, asshole," he growls.

Eirik is already making his way towards the incline to climb up to the assholes that thought they could shoot at us.

"Stay here, don't move." I lean down, taking Freya's lips in a quick kiss before taking off after Eirik. I reach the top in time to see Eirik kick one of the bastards in the shin, but there is no reaction.

"Damn, this is wicked. I love it," he says, grinning at me. "I think I'll shoot these assholes in the nuts, what do you think?"

"We need at least one of them to question so we know why the hell they are following us and now trying to kill us."

Eirik looks at me with a raised brow. "I think that's quite obvious, don't you? Dag is still looking for the woman after they told us not to, that's why."

"Yeah, but I think it's better that we take them back with us. I think there is more to this story than just Dag's mate running. This thing she took with her must be important."

Tor will want payback on the Desperados for trying to kill someone in his charter.

"Fine," Eirik grunts.

"We could drop them, though, on the way down. You know this incline can be slippery," I state which has Eirik grinning.

"I like the way you think," he agrees as he bends down to pick up one of the men and throw him over his shoulder.

"Great minds think alike," I quip as I pick up the other one.

FREYA 14

"You do know that I could have set them free from their statue state, so you didn't need to carry them down, don't you?" My hands are still shaking as my heart races inside my chest. I've never been in a situation like that. Filming a shooting scene and being in one is completely different. I'm still sitting where Dane left me because I don't think my legs will hold me.

Dane suddenly drops the man from his shoulder.

"Dane," I gasp as I see the man fall stiffly to the ground. "Just because he's stiff doesn't mean he won't break something."

"I hope he does," he grunts, which has me shaking my head at him.

"What?" he asks. "These two were trying to kill us."

"Have you ever heard, don't do unto others what you don't want done to you?"

"They were shooting at us, so I guess they are getting off easy." There's no winning with him.

I look over at Anastasia and see her standing over Dag as he leans against the wheel of the van. Ulrich stands behind her with his arms around her waist. What those two did was quite spectacular. To see Ulrich creating fire from nothing, flames that were so hot that I could feel them from where I was sitting, then Anastasia freezing the ground around the fire, it was definitely something that I never thought I would ever see.

I always wondered why I was born with an abnormality, and why everyone around me was normal and I could stop time. There was a time that I thought I was evil because I can do what I do, and when my mom rejected me, I was even more convinced that there was something wrong with me. I kept to myself and tried to be the best person that I could be, I never used my gift unless I thought someone was in danger, which didn't happen much, or when I was angry and it took the best of me.

After each episode, I would feel terrible for days,

thinking that because of my anger, I was letting my evilness overpower me. As the years passed, I just ignored it and forced myself to be as normal as possible, but by then, I was a loner and didn't know how to be anything else. Since meeting the Elementals, I've realized that being different isn't a bad thing—being different is what makes some people special.

When I look at the ground and see some frozen patches still there and the mark of where the fire was, I can only imagine the turmoil that Anastasia must have also gone through when she first found out about what she could do.

"Did you call the cavalry?" Eirik suddenly asks.

"Yeah, I sent Tor a message when this one got injured," Ulrich replies, inclining his head towards Dag. "He's too weak to make it back under his own steam."

"Very funny," Dag mutters. "Unfreeze those assholes and I'll show you how weak I am."

I hear the drone of motorcycles in the distance and wonder if that's what the others were hearing when they asked Ulrich if he contacted the club. A few minutes later the others are pulling up all around us. It is quite an impressive sight when you see all these men approaching. When they are off their bikes, it is clear why other men fear them. The rage that surrounds them because of the attack on us is remarkable.

"Are these the motherfuckers that shot you?" Tor asks, looking at Dag.

"Yeah."

Tor nods, looking at the men on the ground.

"What the fuck is wrong with them?" Colborn asks angrily as he nudges the man that Dane dropped on the ground earlier.

"Freya froze them. Dude, you should have seen it. She just screamed freeze and now look at them," Eirik exclaims, his grin widening as he slaps the back of the man on the ground next to him. Colborn squats in front of the man that is staring off into space. He clicks his fingers in front of the man's face, trying to get a reaction from him. When that doesn't work, he grins and turns towards me.

"Damn, doll, I've got a few people I would like you to do that to."

Dane grunts in annoyance. "She's not entertaining you."

"Chill, Brother, I was just teasing," Colborn says as he stands and turns towards where Tor is now standing with Asger, Ulrich, and Anastasia over Dag.

"Freya, can you undo whatever you did?" Tor asks suddenly as he glances at me. Dane is in the process of helping me up to my feet. I still don't know if my knees won't be banging against each other, but I'll try.

"Unfreeze."

One of the men groans, the one that Dane dropped. He probably broke something.

"How the hell?" the other asks with a surprised look around him.

"Surprised?" Eirik asks.

"Why were you shooting at my men?" Tor growls as he makes his way towards the men, his stealth movements professing to his anger. He gives me the sense of a wild animal closing in on his prey. The men don't answer, they just glare. "I will give you one opportunity to answer. After that, I'm taking the answer from you."

"We have nothing to say, asshole," the one that groaned snaps.

Tor's eyes turn to him and I swear that they are a glacial blue as he squats down before him. "I warned you." His voice is low as his hand snaps out, tightening his hold around the man's upper arm. A minute later the man is gasping and trying to fight his way out of Tor's hold. "I'm waiting." The man screams in pain, as I see smoke and a horrid smell of burnt flesh emanating from him.

"The woman... The woman!" the man cries.

"What woman?"

"He's... after Sean's..." He stops talking and passes out.

Tor pulls his hand away and grunts as he looks down at his bloody hand—blood that belongs to the man he just tortured. He turns to the other man that is looking petrified. I don't blame him I'm petrified and I'm not one of them.

I see Tor raise a brow as he takes a step towards the man. "Sean doesn't . . . doesn't like that. . ." The man is stuttering so badly that his words are hard to understand. "He is looking for... for... for his woman."

"Did he order you to kill Dag?"

The man nods.

"Asger, take the women and Dag back to the club."

My gaze immediately turns to Dane, who takes a step towards me and bends his head down to kiss my forehead.

"It will be fine. I'll see you there." Somehow his words don't appease me as I know that they're probably going to go after Sean. He will probably get arrested for sure now. I shake my head. Maybe if I go with them, I can somehow stop him from doing something that he might regret.

"You might need me," I murmur, which has him suddenly grinning. I don't see where he sees the amusement in the situation. I have just seen a man passing out in pain and Dane is acting as if this is an everyday occurrence.

His fingers stroke my cheek gently. "Trust me, everything will be fine. Now go with Asger before any cars come this way." I didn't even think about traffic. Luckily, there haven't been any cars since we were first ambushed, but what if someone came this way and saw what was happening?

"Okay." I lift up on my tiptoes and kiss his lips once again before stepping back, then I'm walking around Tor, leaving a wide space between me and him. I've always suspected that he was dangerous, but he has just confirmed my suspicions. Tor has been nothing but friendly since we met, but now, I see him in a completely different light. I'm nearly in the van when I feel a hand on my arm, making me cry out in surprise, only to realize that it's Anastasia.

"Sorry, thought you heard me," she says as I slide into the back of the van, Anastasia climbing in next to me.

"No, my mind was miles away," I confess. She takes my hand in hers and squeezes. I don't know if she's trying to comfort me or herself, but I think she's just as shaken as I am with everything that happened today. It started out as a bad day with my mom making an appearance and now this.

No one talks on the drive back. When we arrive, we make our way inside to find Garth and Einar waiting for us. When they see Dag, they both scowl in anger.

"Fuckers. I hope they're dead," Garth grunts.

"Dag, you should go rest," Anastasia says. "I will call Monica to come in and clean the wound for you."

"It's just a scratch, sweetheart."

"Yes, but a scratch can get infected and I'm sure even you can get an infection," Anastasia argues.

"Actually, it will be difficult for him to get an infection," Garth says, but when Anastasia raises a brow at him, he quickly changes his tune. "But it won't kill you to get it clean, maybe Monica can even give you a sponge bath."

That is something else that is completely alien to me, as I've always been a loner, so coming into an environment where women give themselves freely to different men without any emotions involved is something that I will need to get used to. I don't judge them, though. They seem happy and the men treat them really well. What I don't like is the fact that they have been with Dane. Sometimes I wonder if he will compare me to one of them. They must have a lot more experience than me.

The first two weeks, I noticed that Tracy, Monica, and Camille were cautious and at times, purposefully ignoring me, but I think the last week they have warmed up a little. "You might be right. I'm feeling slightly lightheaded all of a sudden," Dag quips.

"Men," Anastasia grumbles. "Come on, Freya. Let's leave the men to their little jokes," Anastasia says as she starts making her way towards the interior of the club.

"Do you know if my mom left a message before she went?" I ask.

"Nope, your mom and the agent left right after you," Garth replies. I can see what looks like pity in his eyes, and I hate the fact that my mom came here. Now everyone will know what kind of relationship I have with my mother. I'm a private person and like to keep my problems and affairs to myself, but I've come to realize that here, everyone knows what is happening, but also, I'm starting to accept that they genuinely care for each other.

"Thank you," I reply as I follow Anastasia. I see that she is waiting for me near the rooms.

"Do you want to go for a swim? I think we can both do with a little chill time."

I would rather just hibernate in my room and think about everything that happened today, but I sense that Anastasia doesn't want to be alone, so I end up agreeing. Half an hour later, I'm entering the pool area to see Anastasia already on the far side, and next to her recliner is a bottle of wine and two glasses.

"Thought we needed more than just the pool to relax,"

she says with a smile as she pours both of us a glass. Sitting down, I sigh as I lean back, stretching out my legs.

"It's actually really pretty in here with all the plants and skylight," I murmur. Picking up the glass, I take a sip of my wine. I look over at Anastasia and see she has her eyes closed, a relaxed look on her face. "Are you okay?"

She turns her head to look at me. "Am I okay? We just saw a man being scorched." Her voice is low, she sounds tired. "No, I don't like the fact that the men have to fight or resort to other means to protect themselves and us. I'm also not okay with being shot at today." She sighs as she turns her head and closes her eyes again.

"Is it always like that?" The thought of what I saw still turns my stomach, the stench of his burning flesh still hovering in my nostrils.

"No, luckily it's not."

"What is going to happen now?"

She shrugs. Lifting her hand, she takes a sip of her wine before looking at me again. "Now they go and employ their revenge on the Desperados for having injured one of them, and for having placed two of their women in harm's way."

The thought of Dane in a situation where there will be

shooting has my stomach knotting. From what I saw today, I know that the men have powers beyond my imagination, and that they can take care of themselves, but I still worry. I think that Dane and I need to practice in harmonizing our two gifts like I saw Anastasia do with Ulrich. If there is a situation where we must do it once again and combine our powers, I'd like to know if we can work together like I saw the other couple do.

DANE 15

"That fucker thinks he can send his men after us. We are confronting him now, and we will take his puppets with us," Tor orders as his gaze bores into us, his anger palpable. We have parked our bikes out of the way and are waiting for Garth to bring the SUV so we can take the men we captured with us and offer them to Sean as a lesson of what will happen to anyone that attacks us.

"He wouldn't go to such lengths just to get a woman back. There must be more here besides Esmeralda stealing from him. He doesn't want anyone else to talk to her before he gets his hands on her. Therefore, we will all be out there now looking for her. Not just because he attacked us, but also because she's Dag's mate." Tor's tone professes to his determination—a determination that we all know way too well. If he sets his mind on something, then we know that he will get it.

"Dag phoned Draco today to get his mate's help in locating Esmeralda," Eirik says.

"Good. He must have sent Draco an image of that photo of her that he has," Tor states. "Katrina will find her soon."

"That's a handy gift to have," Colborn says from where he's leaning against a tree.

"I'm fucking impressed with your woman's gift, I've never seen someone freeze like that before," Eirik says, turning to me. "Damn, she saved my fucking life. Do you know that she froze a bullet just feet from my fucking head?"

"Looks like you have competition, Dane," Colborn teases.

I know that Eirik is thankful and impressed with Freya's gift. Shit, I am too. I'm proud of the way she handled herself and held together through everything. I wish I could be with her right now. I could feel her shaking when I helped her up. But being part of our Chapter, she will need to get used to these situations sometimes, even though I fucking hope they don't happen often when the women are around.

I know that Eirik is impressed with Freya's gift, but I know that he would never try anything with another brother's old lady. Also because she's my mate, he knows that he would never have a chance with her no matter what.

"Draco's men always brag about how unique their women are. Well, boys, I think we have some really impressive gifts in our women too," Ulrich states with a wide smile.

"I think that I can enhance Freya's gift," I say.

This has Tor and the others looking at me.

"When she tried to freeze the men initially, they didn't because her command didn't reach them. I'm guessing it's her voice that gives her the power to do what she does. I used the wind to carry her voice up to the men. I think that she would freeze large areas if we required it."

"That's good to know," Tor says as he raises his hand to his chin, rubbing the stubble there. "We need to see if she can do the same to the Keres." Now that would be interesting, because if she can freeze the Keres there have been various times that we have rooted them out and know that they are somewhere, but when we arrive, they have sensed us and escaped.

If somehow Freya can freeze them from a distance, we might be able to catch them before they have a chance to escape.

"Does her gift work if people are deaf, or wearing ear protectors?" Tal asks. "You said that it seems to be her voice that has the power. Maybe if the people protect their hearing, they won't be affected."

That is a good question. "I will ask her, but if she doesn't know then we will have to test it," I say just as Garth pulls up in the SUV. About time. I want to get this party on the road and get back to my woman. She has clearly never been in a situation like the one today, I hope she doesn't freak out and decide that this life isn't for her after all, because there is no way that mates can be apart.

"I knew you guys couldn't do this without me." Garth says with a grin as he steps out of the SUV to walk towards the assholes that are sitting behind one of the trees, so no one sees them if they drive past. Colborn is keeping an eye on them, and we can also hear if they move.

"Nope, we just needed a driver," Ulrich quips as he walks towards Garth with a grin on his face.

"I think Garth is going to need someone to keep an eye on those fuckers in the SUV. You can go with him, Ulrich," Tor says after Ulrich's chirp, which has him grunting, and Garth chuckling.

"Guess you can drive back," Garth says in good humour as he picks one of the assholes up by his lapels and drags him towards the back of the SUV. The rest of us get onto our bikes and prepare to make our way to confront Sean and his men. He won't be expecting us, but he should have thought about that when he decided to attack us and injure one of our men.

Garth pulls away with the men and the rest of us follow behind. We make our way towards where we know Sean usually hangs out, but we know that the area is always crawling with his men. It will be tricky getting close to him, but we will. I would love nothing more than to squeeze the breath out of the son of a bitch for putting my woman in danger, but we will see how it goes.

If Tor decides the fucker needs to be killed, then we will, but that means war with the Desperados, because I know that they would retaliate if we killed their leader. When we are a couple blocks away, we start seeing some of Sean's men in the area. By the comments we hear as we ride past, we know that they're in contact with Sean. When we get to him, he will be waiting.

Pulling up outside a restaurant that Sean and his men operate out of, we switch off our bikes and wait for Ulrich and Garth to pull the semi-conscious men out of the back of the SUV and dump them at the restaurant's door. There is only one display window to the restaurant. From that window I can see Sean making his way towards the entrance. Two of his men flank him, but riding up, I could see at least fifteen men standing around trying to blend into the background, ready to attack us if Sean orders them to.

"What is this?" Sean asks in an angry voice when he sees the men's state.

"At least they're still breathing. That's more than you ordered for my man if they had got their way," Tor says in a calm voice. Anyone that knows Tor would know that when he's calm, he's at his most dangerous.

"He was warned to stop looking for my woman," Sean states, not making an effort to help his wounded men.

"I thought you would be pleased that Dag was helping you find your woman," Tor states.

"We don't need your man's help; we will find her on our own," Sean informs him as he places his hands on his hips. "Tell him to stop looking or next time he won't leave breathing."

His threat against Dag makes me still. This motherfucker thinks he can threaten one of us and we will take it without any retaliation.

"I'm afraid that won't be possible," Tor says in a friendly tone, but everyone can hear the underlying danger in his voice.

Sean scowls at Tor's statement, his face flushing in

anger.

"You see, Sean, now you spiked our curiosity, and all of my men will now be out looking for her."

"This has nothing to do with you!" Sean grunts in anger.

"I'm afraid it does. The minute you decided to shoot one of my men, endangering two of our women, it became all of our business," Tor states.

"You are willing to go to war for a woman you don't even know?" Sean growls.

"No, but I'm willing to go to war for my man, which you ordered to be shot, and the two women which lives were endangered at the time of the shooting."

"This is crazy, Tor, he was warned."

Tor shrugs at Sean's statement.

"If we find any of your men snooping around my woman, we will have to stop them."

"You do what you think you should, but be warned that the next time any of your men engages one of mine, they will be dead." With that statement Tor leans forward and starts his bike. The roar of his Harley is followed by all our others. Garth and Ulrich pull away in the SUV, then the rest of us follow. The warning has been given, it is now open season and if we come across any of the Desperados, they will be dead. We make our way out of the Desperado's area and back towards the club. From now on, we need to be careful where and how we go out.

The Elementals Cape Town Chapter has declared war with the Desperados. We will be riding in a group from now on, and we will be armed, because even though we could disperse any of them without any weapons, we try not to use our gifts in public. If we do, we make sure that there are no witnesses left behind that can retell what they saw.

Parking the bikes outside our club, most of the men start making their way inside before Tor stops them. "Church in ten," he grunts as he strides inside as if a war wasn't just declared between the club and a Cape Town gang. Fuck, I was hoping to go and talk to Freya because I want to make sure that she's okay after what she witnessed today.

Flexing my shoulders, I make my way inside and towards the meeting room. I will go to Freya as soon as the meeting is over. I can sense that she is okay, therefore, there is no hurry to rush to her side.

We all start taking our seats around the table, as soon as all the men are in, the door is closed, and Tor sits back in his chair with a watchful look in his eyes as he gazes around the table at all of us before talking. "We haven't been at war for a while now, not since most of the Keres were captured. Most of us have grown lax with the peace, but today we are at war again, and not just any war, but a war with one of Cape Town's most dangerous gangs. From now on, we have eyes everywhere. I want to know what they are doing at all times," Tor states in anger. "If they take a pee, I want to know about it." Motherfuckers, because of them I'm going to spend minimal time with Freya.

"Dag, how are you?" Tor asks.

"I've been better, but it's only a scratch. The fuckers can't even get killing someone right," he states.

"Don't be cocky. You could have been killed if you were by yourself," Tor reminds him with a scowl.

"Those fuckers couldn't hit an elephant if it was in front of them," Dag encourages with a grin.

"Not all of them are like that," Asgar says as he sits forward, placing his folded hands before him on the table. "Some men are actually decent shots. I know some of them practice quite often at a plot that Sean owns just out of Cape Town."

"From this point forward, you are all to go out in groups. There are no exceptions." There are a few grunts of annoyance, but no one contradicts Tor's orders. We all know when there is a war, we all need to keep our wits about us and draw together because only if we move as one will we conquer our enemies. We have been together for centuries; we know how to fight in unison like a well-oiled machine.

"We need to find Dag's woman fast because they will leave no stone unturned, and we want to get to her before they do."

"Fuckers," Dag snaps in anger. "I swear they are fucking leeches, because every time I turn around there is one of those assholes following me."

"Do you think they will get the other gangs involved in this war?" Garth asks.

"They might, so be prepared if you see anyone that is part of a gang," Tor instructs us.

"Are you going to inform Draco that we are at war with the Desperados gang?" Colborn asks, which has Tor tense and scowl as we all know that Draco is not going to be happy about the Elementals being at war again.

"Eventually," Tor grumbles, which has me grinning in amusement when I think of that conversation. Draco, the Elementals MC National President, is not someone that likes to be disobeyed. When it comes to our Chapter, it looks like we can't help ourselves because we always seem to do something that contradicts what the main chapter states.

"Ulrich, you and Dane need to keep track of your women from now until this war is finished, we are on lockdown," Tor informs us.

"Fuck, Anastasia is going to freak," Ulrich mumbles which have some of the others grin in amusement at his grumbling, but I understand where he's coming from as I doubt that Freya is going to love the idea of not being able to get out of the club for a while.

FREYA 16

"This is driving me crazy! I can't sit here any longer." I look up from the seeds I'm planting towards where Anastasia is sitting. She has been holding her Kindle for the last hour, but I've noticed that her eyes were everywhere but on the book that she was supposed to be reading.

"Do you want to help me?" I ask.

"Planting?" Anastasia looks at me in surprise, as if I asked her to parade naked around the garden.

"Yes."

She shakes her head. "No thanks, I just need to get out

of the club for a little while." I know that she's going crazy from being locked inside for the last two weeks, but the men are adamant about us not going out. "I know it's dangerous at the moment, but I'm sure that if we just nip out to the store that no one will know who the hell we are."

I sigh. She has been trying to get me to go out with her for a couple days, but to no avail. I must be honest, the thought that after two weeks of being at the club without being able to leave is starting to stress me out too.

I'm someone that doesn't mind being alone in my own company at home, but even I start to feel claustrophobic. "Maybe if we ask the men to take us out, they will, even if it's just for a little while."

"I asked Ulrich last night. He said no and that it was too dangerous," Anastasia says in a sarcastic tone. "I hate it when he does that. It's too dangerous for us but not too dangerous for them." She's irritated today, and I don't think that irritation is going to get any better until she goes out. "It wouldn't be as bad if the men weren't gone for so long."

I know what she means. I've hardly spent any time with Dane in these last two weeks. It's frustrating that I can feel he's irritated with the situation, but there is nothing that any of us can do, not until they find this woman they are looking for. Dane told me that apparently, she's Dag's mate, and no matter what, they're going to have to find her because she's in danger.

They were hopeful a couple days ago when Katrina, Draco's mate, told them that she knew where the woman they are looking for is, but the problem was that when they got close, she managed to escape them. Dane says that they missed her by an hour at the most because they could still sense her energy when they got there.

Last night when Dane came back, he was wired, something happened that had flustered his temper. When he got to our room, he hardly talked, he just started kissing me and caressing me. He made love to me like a man on a mission. Thoroughly, passionately, and all consuming. There is nothing about Dane that I would change, even his troglodyte actions sometimes. He makes me feel like no one ever has, and he makes me feel loved even though he has never told me he loves me. Deep down, I know that he does.

"I'm going into town and you are coming with me."

I frown. What did I miss? I was so distracted with my thoughts that I missed Anastasia's ranting until now.

"We can't," I say, looking behind her to make sure that no one heard her. "It's dangerous."

"If we don't wear the kuttes, we will be fine. No one will know that we are Elemental's old ladies." I want to go out even if just for an hour, but what if we are wrong and they do know that we belong to them?

"I don't know, Anastasia. I don't think the men will like the fact that we are going out."

Anastasia shrugs at my words. "That's the point. Don't you want to be naughty sometimes?"

I don't know what Dane will do if I contradict his request and go out. I don't want to upset him, but he hasn't tried to take me out during these two weeks. He can't expect us to live here indefinitely until this war ends with the Desperados.

"Okay, but how are we going to make it out of here without anyone noticing?" I know that the club is on lockdown—no one is allowed in or out without the men knowing about it. The prospects are usually on guard while most of the men are out looking for this woman that belongs to Dag.

"We walk out," Anastasia says with a grin. "I have my car keys. We stroll out of the club, get into the car, then we drive right through the gates."

I raise my brows in question. It looks like she has been planning this for a while. "The main gates have been closed if you haven't noticed." Since this war was declared, I've noticed that the prospects have the gates always closed unless the men are coming in or out.

"We have a small window of opportunity. When the prospects walk up the road to get the post, they leave the gate open. We can drive past without them being able to do anything."

That just makes me nervous. "If we do that, the prospects will be on the phone with one of the men before we can make it to the end of the road. Then, instead of them concentrating on what they are doing, they will be after us."

She frowns. "Well, what do you suggest?"

"What if we don't take your car and catch the bus?"

She looks at me curiously. "And how do we get out to catch the bus?"

"I'm sure we can find the key to the gate somewhere." The property has a side gate that is always locked, but the key must be somewhere inside, in case someone needs to leave through the gate. If we can slip out of the gate, then we should be able to make it to the bus stop and into town before anyone is the wiser.

"Oh, why didn't I think of that?" Anastasia says with a smile on her face. I think it's the first smile I've seen on her face today. "I know where that key is, the trick is to get in and pick it up."

"Where is it?"

"Tor keeps a key on the top drawer of his desk, but I

don't know if he went out with the men today or if he's in his office," she says biting her bottom lip.

"He went out. I saw him leaving earlier with Eirik and Einar."

She claps her hands, standing up from the bench she has been sitting on since this morning.

"Well, what are we waiting for?" she says with a smile. "Let's go get that key and what we need before he comes back."

I'm still wary about what can happen, but I'm sure I can stop time if required so the two of us can escape if need be. "Fine, I'll go and change quickly as my jeans have soil stains and meet you by the back door. Will you get the key, or do you want me to come with you to check if anyone is coming?"

Anastasia shakes her head. "No need, if you stand around outside Tor's office it will be suspicious, and then someone is bound to come investigate."

I nod as I follow her inside. She makes her way towards Tor's office while I head to Dane's and my room. Now that we have a plan, I'm excited. I know that we were warned to stay inside, but as Anastasia said, no one will know that we belong to the Elementals if we don't wear the kutte. Besides, I'm used to dressing to hide my appearance as people always tend to stop me when I go out.

Opening one of my bags that I haven't opened since arriving at the club. I pull out a blond wig that I used to distract people from who I am. Then I pull on a fresh pair of jeans and a baggy hoodie before looking in the mirror and smiling as I place a cap on my head. I just need to get my contacts on and then I'm ready to go out. Even though I don't have a problem with anyone at the club seeing my eyes any longer, I still feel uncomfortable out in public. It feels like I'm naked for everyone to see.

I've hidden my eyes for so long that now, without my contacts, I feel vulnerable. Making my way towards the door which we agreed to meet at, I wait for Anastasia, hoping no one comes along and finds it strange that I'm just hanging around looking like I do. Five minutes later, I'm thinking of walking towards Ulrich and Anastasia's room when I see her making her way towards me.

When she sees my appearance, she grins. "Damn, I didn't recognize you at first," she says as she opens the door. "Tor had the drawer locked. It was harder to get the key than I thought."

"So how did you get it?"

I see Anastasia's cheek darken with colour as she looks at me. "I broke into the drawer."

"Oh my word, Tor is not going to be happy," I grumble. I don't want to be in her shoes if she faces Tor, but to be fair, this was my plan, so if he gets upset, it is as much my fault as it is hers.

We make our way towards the gate. Anastasia slots the key into the keyhole and then struggles to turn it. "It's stuck," she grumbles.

"Let me try." Not that I'm stronger than her, but it can't hurt. We didn't come this far to now have to turn back.

It takes a couple of minutes of jiggling and trying to lift the gate before we both make it to the other side. "Do you know where the bus stop is?" Only now do I realize that I suggested the bus, but I have no idea if the bus drives past the club or anywhere close.

"Yes, it's just two blocks away," Anastasia says as she pulls her arm through mine, making our way towards the bus stop.

"I can't believe we are doing this," I say with a laugh. "They are going to be so angry when they find out." I hope Dane isn't too angry, but I've never done something like this before. I've never had a friend that I could be a rebel with, and this feels so exciting.

"It's okay, they will get over it," Anastasia says just as we see a bus in the distance driving towards us. "Oh, we need to run, or we won't make it."

We take off towards the bus stop, arriving just as the bus pulls up.

"Now this was perfect timing," I say as I gasp for breath,

following Anastasia to the back of the bus and sitting. The bus is almost empty, which is good. I haven't been on a bus in years. This is a new experience for me, which I'm enjoying as I look at the other passengers. I love people watching. Sometimes it's even more exciting to look at than the scenery for me.

Anastasia is now all smiles as we make our way into town. She chats the whole way, but to be honest I'm not really listening as I look around at everyone, smiling at a little boy that is sitting next to his mom eating an ice-cream. Will that be me one day? Will I have Dane's babies? I haven't been curious about it until now. Is it possible for humans to have children with Elementals? I'm guessing that if we are their mates, then we should be compatible, but I've learned never to assume.

"Can we have children with them?" I interrupt Anastasia, which has her look at me in surprise.

"Where did that come from?" she asks.

I shrug, not sure myself why the thought popped into my mind. Do I want children with Dane? I've never really thought about having children. My career didn't seem like the best profession to have children with, and I hadn't really met anyone that I liked enough to take such a big step. But now that I met Dane, that has all changed. I don't have to worry about having to fly all around the world for work or that I will never meet someone that I love. I hadn't thought about it before.

How did it happen so fast? I know that I was infatuated with Dane, I mean who wouldn't be? But I hadn't thought it was love, yet. Is it just the bond we have, or do I really love him?

"Yes, we can have children with them as the women that I've met from the Elementals Mother Chapter have children."

That means that I could be pregnant right now because we haven't done anything for contraception. I feel my heart racing when I think of a little Dane running around and me as a mom. Will I be a good mom?

"Our stop," Anastasia suddenly says as she stands.

We make our way out of the bus and towards the shops. "Are you pregnant?" Anastasia suddenly asks, a frown on her face.

"No, I was just curious," I say with a smile.

"Apparently, it happens when it has to happen. Nova, one of the other mates, told me that it doesn't matter what contraception you use, it doesn't work with the Elementals."

I wasn't going to use any contraception, but that is interesting to know. "Oh, let's go in there," I say as we see a nice little rustic coffee shop just ahead.

"Yes, please," Anastasia replies. "I've wanted a nice piece of chocolate cake. I haven't had it in such a long time, I really hope they have something decadent inside. I might even have two slices," she quips as we walk inside.

This must be a popular little coffee shop. The tables are all occupied. I sigh in annoyance as I just wanted to sit down and enjoy a nice cup of coffee and a slice of cake. "Maybe we can sit at that table, if she's alone I'm sure she won't mind." I look towards the far corner and see a woman sitting there. I can't see her face because she is leaning back in the shadows.

"We can try." I'm not someone that would just go up to someone and ask if I can sit at their table, but today is a first time for everything, so I might as well try this too.

I follow Anastasia and see the woman tense as we approach.

"Hi, do you mind if we sit with you?" Anastasia asks, sending her a friendly smile. "All the tables are full, and all we wanted was a cup of coffee and a treat."

Up close, I can see the woman has pitch black hair and very light green eyes. She seems reluctant, her eyes traveling around the coffee shop and then over us before she nods.

"Oh, thank you."

We take our seats and smile, but I see that she seems uncomfortable with this interruption.

"I'm Freya, this is Anastasia," I say, introducing us. "Thank you for letting us join you. As a thank you, I would like to offer to pay for your coffee."

I see a look of surprise in her eyes, but then she nods. "Thank you."

"We are actually being naughty today," Anastasia says. "We're not supposed to be out and about, our men are not going to be happy when they find out."

The woman has a look of shock on her face, her whole body going rigid.

"It's just that they went out and don't know that we have come out too, they will be worried." For some reason I think this woman is hiding something, but I have no idea what it could be. All I know is what my senses are telling me, and they are saying that she's in pain, but I don't think it's a physical pain, more of a mental or even spiritual pain.

"Have you tried the chocolate cake here? All I want is a slice of decadent chocolate cake."

Anastasia's question has her smiling as she nods. "That is why I come here; they have the best chocolate cake I've ever tasted." Well, it looks like Anastasia and this woman have found something in common—they are both chocoholics. I personally prefer a carrot cake, or something fruity. The waitress takes our order just as my phone starts ringing.

Taking the phone out of my haversack, which I brought with me just in case I want to buy anything, I see that it's Dane phoning. Oh boy, does he know yet? "It's Dane," I say before answering. "Hello?"

"Hey, baby cheeks." Dane has got into the habit of calling me different pet names. I think that if he knew we had slipped away; he wouldn't be so understanding. "Just wanted to let you know that. . ." he stops suddenly, there is silence on the line before he speaks again. "Where are you?" Damn, he must have heard the other clients talking in the background.

"Don't be angry. Anastasia and I were tired of being locked up. We are being safe, so don't worry."

"What the fuck," I hear him roar, which has me pulling the phone slightly away from my ear. I guess me saying that we are safe hasn't appeased his anger. Anastasia nudges me. Glancing over at her, I see her indicate for me to disconnect the call, but I shake my head. I won't do that. It's not right to have him worry unnecessarily.

"Seriously, don't worry. We are being safe, and no one knows who we are," I soothe him and see the woman at our table raise her brows at my words.

"Where are you?" His voice is low, and I can hear the anger vibrating in each word.

"We came into town." I don't want to say where we are just yet, as I know that one of the men will be here to collect us before we can have our coffee. "I have to go. I will let you know when we are on our way back."

"Freya!" I hear him roar, but I disconnect the call.

"He didn't sound happy..." the woman says with a watchful look.

"He's just worried because the Elementals are having some problems with a gang; he just wants to make sure we are safe."

"I've heard of the Elementals; they seem to be an MC to be afraid of," the woman says.

"Oh, they are, but they don't believe in hurting women or children. That is why they are at war with the gang, apparently they are looking for a woman that ran away from them and the men are worried that she will be killed when found."

"You mean that they have gone to war because of a woman they don't know?"

I nod at her words as Anastasia answers. "Of course, what kind of men would they be if they knew someone was in trouble and did nothing to help?"

I can see the suspicious look on her face, but she shrugs, asking instead. "How will they stop it? After all, I've heard these street gangs are dangerous."

"I'm not sure yet, but they will find away," I say just as

our cake arrives, turning to take my plate I see the woman bend to pick something up from the ground, but when I turn back with my cake, she is standing.

"Enjoy your cake, thank you for the coffee. I have to go."

I smile as we say our goodbyes, watching her walk out. Something about her is still teasing me, but for the life of me, I don't know what it is.

"Now that they know we are not home, we better hurry up and eat because I'm sure either Ulrich or Dane will be here soon," Anastasia says with a big smile as she takes a bite out of her cake. "Mmm, so good," she murmurs in pleasure.

"I didn't tell Dane where we are, so I'm sure we will have a little time."

Anastasia glances at me in surprise and shakes her head. "It will just take them the time from wherever they are to here, so if it's ten minutes or an hour, that's how long it will take." She glances around, then back to me as she lowers her voice. "As their mates, they can find us anywhere." I know about them being able to find their mates, I just didn't think it was that quick.

I'm still eating my cake and drinking my coffee when I hear bikes outside. "Oh well, at least we had a nice cup of coffee and some cake," Anastasia laughs as she leans back and takes a sip of her coffee.

I hear the door to the coffee shop open and the conversation in the establishment dies down, telling me that one of the Elementals has just walked in, but I don't turn to look. "Get ready," Anastasia says with a wink just as Ulrich slides into the seat before us, his expression thunderous, Dane is right behind him taking a seat after him.

"Anastasia, what the hell do you think you were doing?" His displeasure is palpable.

"I didn't expect this from you," Dane says as he picks up my fork to take a bite of my cake.

"We're not doing anything wrong. We just came for coffee and a slice of cake," I answer with a shrug.

"Nothing wrong?" Dane grumbles. "If any of the Desperados found you, they would be taking you, or hurting you, just to prove a point."

"Surely not. Besides, they wouldn't recognize me, anyway."

Dane's eyes roam over my appearance. I can hear Ulrich and Anastasia arguing, but Dane is the one that interests me at this moment.

"You did disguise yourself quite well to be fair," Dane says as he lifts his hand to lift a strand of the wig between his fingers to examine it.

"That is besides the point, they could have seen the two

of you leaving the club. We don't know if someone is keeping an eye on the club," Ulrich argues.

"We left through the side gate, I'm sure no one is watching that," Anastasia says before taking another sip of her coffee.

"How the hell did you get the keys for the side gate?"

"Well, umm," Anastasia says, throwing me a wide-eyed look over her coffee.

"We got it from Tor's drawer," I tell them, not saying that Anastasia broke into the drawer to get the key.

"Damn, like it wasn't bad enough that you purposefully disobeyed us, but now you also went into his drawer?" Ulrich snaps as he lifts his hand to pull his fingers through his hair. "He's going to be livid."

"The women are fine," Dane says, "he will get over it."

"Sure, he will, after he has a go at us," Ulrich argues.

"He's going to argue with you?" Why would he argue with the men when it isn't their fault?

"You should be safe and you're not. You placed yourselves in danger. You are both our responsibility. As our mates, you are supposed to listen to what we say and not purposefully disobey us." Oh, I didn't know that I would be getting Dane in trouble because of this.

"I'm sorry," I murmur as I look at Dane.

"We can't be locked in the club, without any outside interaction," Anastasia argues. "It's like being in prison."

Ulrich throws up his hands in irritation. "Damn, woman. It's dangerous out here. You have everything you want inside the club, what could you possibly need?"

"This chocolate cake for one."

"The point is that we can't be locked inside indefinitely. You need to understand that we need to get out every now and again."

"That's not possible at the moment," Ulrich says.

"Wait," Dane suddenly responds before Anastasia has a chance to argue again. "We can try, but Ulrich isn't being difficult. Things are heating up fast and if we're not careful, they will get to you." Glancing back, I see that people are starting to look at us.

"We should go," I murmur, bringing the other's attention to the people in the coffee shop.

"Yeah," Dane says, standing, as he moves towards the counter to pay. I lean down to pick up my haversack, only to see that it's open. Did I leave it open? Looking inside, I frown when I see a hard-covered notebook inside that isn't mine. Pulling it out, I open the book to see a lot of names, figures, and dates. I flip to another page in the middle and tense. What the hell is this?

"Dane." I call as I stand making my way towards him. "Look what I found in my haversack." I hand him the book after he slips the change into his pocket. Frowning, he takes the book and opens it. A minute later his whole body stills.

"Where the fuck did you get this?"

"I think the girl we were sitting with slipped it into my bag before she left." I see his eyes widen before he pulls the haversack off my shoulder, placing the book back inside he closes it before slipping it onto his own shoulder.

"Ulrich, let's go," he orders as he grabs the top of my arm, guiding me out of the coffee shop and towards the two bikes. I don't know what's in that book, but he seems determined to leave even sooner than before.

DANE 17

We have been looking all over and she was fucking sitting in a coffee shop?" Dag asks while he paces the room.

I didn't believe it when Freya handed me a book with dates, times, and notes of things that have transpired between the Desperados and other gangs. We haven't gone through the whole book yet, but we might even have information of which Keres is organizing the abduction of women with gifts like Anastasia and Freya who are being trafficked into Dubai and other countries.

"Why didn't you keep her there?"

I know he's frustrated at how long it's taken to find his

woman, but berating our women for something that they didn't even know is not acceptable.

"Dag," I warn. I will not have him raise his voice at Freya.

He grunts before he nods.

"We didn't know she was the woman you were looking for," Anastasia says as she sits back against Ulrich's chest. He pulled her into his lap the minute we walked into the bar. Looks like they have resolved their argument.

"She seemed slightly nervous, but she gave no indication that she was running away from anyone. If anything, she looked quite calm," Freya says from the chair next to mine.

Tor and Asgar are looking through the book at the moment, and every now and then, I see them discuss something they see.

"No wonder he's got all his men after her. He has noted every single thing they have done as a club," Asgar mutters.

"Asshole," Colborn says as he walks towards the bar to pick up a beer.

"Bring me one," I ask while stroking Freya's neck. My arm is behind her chair, my hand caressing her smooth skin. Colborn hands me the beer and then walks to take a seat next to Garth.

"I think she gave me the book so that you can stop the Desperados," Freya says with a frown. "When we mentioned that you wanted to stop them from hurting women and children, she was very interested. Right after that she left."

"We need to find her. Did she say anything about where she is staying?" Dag asks.

"No, Dag, she didn't," Anastasia replies.

"Guys, I think he has info here about the Keres," Tor states as he continues to page through the book. "He talks in here about meeting Aldor, and that this Aldor is not someone to play with. They can get everything they ever wanted if they can find who they are looking for."

"Does it say anything about where they meet or how they know which women they need to find?" Tal asks.

"There are coordinates here, I think these coordinates are for where they drop off the women," Asgar says out loud.

"Looks like your woman helped us more than she thinks," Einar says to Dag.

"We need to find Esmeralda and bring her in. She needs to know that she will be safe here," Dag says.

"We mentioned to her that we are with the Elementals

and that you guys are decent and want what's right. Maybe she will show up one of these days at the gate asking for help," Freya suggests before glancing at me.

"I think that she wants proof that we will do something to stop the Desperados before she makes an appearance," Anastasia adds.

"Colborn, check these coordinates out. I want to know what and where they are for." Colborn pulls out his phone as he leans towards the desk to look at the coordinates before he inputs them into his phone.

"It's downtown," he reveals with a frown on his face as he scratches his jaw while looking at the screen. "I'm not sure what this is about, but look at which building the coordinates are for." Turning the phone, he shows it to everyone. The building that he is showing us belongs to a multimillion-dollar corporation. Is it possible that the Keres are involved with that corporation? If that is the case, then we have more to worry about than we thought because we will have to bring others in to help. There is a lot of money involved, if the Keres have any connection there.

"Shit," Tal snaps as he sits forward. "I will contact Celmund to look into them and see what he can find." Celmund is our best tech guy and a hacker in his own right. If you need to know anything, usually Celmund can find what we are looking for with very little information, like the name of a building and coordinates.

I just want some peace to spend time with my mate, it feels like ever since we met that everything has gone to hell, with one thing or another. Now that she's starting to settle in, it seems like I'm the one that is never here as we are constantly on the road either looking for Esmeralda or acquiring information about the Desperados to try to stop them.

Standing, I see Freya's surprised look as I take her hand. "I'm tired and after the exciting day the two of you had, I'm sure you are tired too," I say to Freya as I help her out of her chair. "See you in the morning," I call to everyone, as Freya says her goodnights before she walks with me to our room.

Closing the door behind us, I look at my woman as she approaches the bed before taking a seat to look at me. "Are you angry with me?" she asks.

"Yes," I reply gruffly. She needs to know that I have to be able to trust her to do as I say, or I won't be able to concentrate when I need to.

"I'm sorry, but being locked up twenty-four seven is not something that Anastasia and I are used to." Her hands are on her lap and I notice her fingers twisting the fabric of her T-shirt in anxiety. I don't want my woman to feel anxious about this, but I need her to be aware that I will only ask things of her when they are important.

"I need to be able to know that when I ask you something that you will do what I ask because otherwise, we are going to have a problem." Approaching her, I squat down . "If you had spoken to me about wanting to go out, I would have made a plan."

"I told you I was tired of being locked up here," she says with a frown.

Lifting my hand, I smooth the frown lines away as I lean forward to kiss her lips. "I know, but I didn't think you were that fed up. Next time make me listen or be more direct and tell me exactly what you want," I tell her, wanting to make sure that she is completely open with me.

"Like telling you that I want you to kiss me?"

I nod at her comparison, then notice her raised brow, realizing that she is telling me she wants me to kiss her right now. Grinning, I lean forward. She doesn't need to ask me twice to kiss her. Placing my hand behind her neck, I pull her towards me as I lean forward, taking her lips in a blistering kiss while I run my fingers through her hair before pulling it into a knot at the back, making sure she doesn't move her head as I overwhelm her with all the passion coursing through me.

Her murmurs of pleasure drive my desire even higher, my body tensing in readiness to take my woman through every erotic thought that I've ever had. My other hand strokes over her ribcage while my thumb rubs just under her perfect breast. Our tongues step around each other in a dance older than time—a passionate tango of the senses.

Her hands wrap around my neck as she surrenders to the passion that is building between us. Letting go of her hair, I bring my hand down her body, taking hold of the hem of her T-shirt to pull it up with one yank. Her nipples peep out at me through her lacy bra—rosy pebbles peaked in readiness for my kisses. I feel her hands wandering down my chest, stroking over my abdomen before they roam under my T-shirt, her fingers caressing my skin like a spark of electricity that charges my senses—a storm igniting a bolt of lightning in the sky.

I raise my hands up to her breasts. Fisting my fingers around the lacy fabric, I pull it down, exposing her erect nipples. The lusciousness has my mouth watering in anticipation as I lower my head to take one rosy nipple between my lips, sucking to heighten her arousal. Her hands go to my T-shirt to pull it up, tugging it away from my body. My hardness fights for its release, as my jeans strangle its pulsing length. Her nails scratch down the length of my torso, my muscles rippling in readiness. Her fingers stop at the top button of my low-cut jeans. When the first one pops, I hold my breath, waiting to feel her gentle touch. When she finally gets to the last button, my shaft springs out in readiness.

Her fingers run along my length to the base, her head

lowering as she kisses the tip of my erection. An overwhelming feeling of belonging is caused by the caresses of my woman, exposing my full-blown desire for her that's ignited by her gentle touch, bringing me to my knees with all her passionate actions. My hardness pulsates in her hand as her fingers circle its girth, tugging at the explosion that is bubbling just under the surface.

My hands move down to unbutton her jeans, lips still playing, kissing, and tugging at her nipples. Fisting the waist of the jeans, I tug down, pulling them off her legs, exposing her red lacy panties and her mound calling for my touch. My hardness is throbbing. Each stroke of her hand brings me closer to my pinnacle. Pulling away from her hand, I step back, discarding my jeans and boots. When I look up, Freya has taken her panties off and is lying on the bed looking at me.

"You are so beautiful," I murmur as I place my knee on the bed next to her. My eyes travel over her body, her silky skin glistening in the light. Freya lifts her hands, placing them over her breasts, squeezing them gently, the nipples peaking between her fingers. The absolute perfection of the moment has my eyes transfixed on her movements. I want nothing more than to touch her, but to see her touching herself has me pausing—observing.

This woman before me has my blood coursing through my body like molten lava; the heat threatening to erupt before I can even touch her like I want to. I let her tease me for another minute or two before I take command. Placing my hand on her knee, I widen it as I slot myself between her legs on my knees. My eyes travel her majestic temple of a body. Leaning down, I kiss her navel, my lips teasing her bellybutton. Her legs rise as she encircles my back, her hands sliding into my hair as she pulls gently while I kiss down her body slowly, wandering my way down to her womanhood, to the heat of her very core. When my lips touch her, she gasps lifting her pelvis, my hands move under her ass holding her up.

My tongue darts between her lips, tasting her sweetness as her body pulses with passion. She gasps, her moans intensifying with each stroke of my tongue. Her legs stiffen as I bring her closer to the point of no return. Lifting my head, I place my hand over her sensitive mound, stroking my fingers gently over her swollen nub. My middle finger penetrates her heat, stroking her passion to a frenzied climax.

My body craves release as I see her quivering in ecstasy. I begin kissing my way up her body until I'm quieting her gasps with my kisses, my pulsing shaft finding her spasming heat. Penetrating with one deep thrust, Freya gasps. My movements intensify with each thrust, kisses deepening with each moment of passion that we share. My penetrating thrusts speed up as my vision focuses on Freya, her beauty beyond anything I could have imagined when I thought of my mate.

"Dane," she gasps as I pull her legs up until her ankles are resting on my shoulder, her hips raise so that my thrusts are deeper, harder, and all consuming. Her breathing becomes shallow as her body tightens, her inner muscles gripping my shaft with such intensity that I feel myself losing control. My mind is consumed with this moment, blanking everything around me except the woman beneath me.

This woman is everything I could ever want, she blows my mind with her passion, my body with ecstasy, and my soul with love. "Freya," I roar as my release overtakes me. I feel my release explode, my very essence coating deep within her body. I feel spent, completely, and utterly drained. Something that I don't usually feel because our bond has consumed me, knitting our two souls, and making it one.

"You have completely exhausted me, woman," I murmur as I slip out of her.

Freya smiles, her eyes closed with a content look on her face. "If you are exhausted, then I'm dead," she whispers, "but living in heaven." Her words have me grinning as I lie on my back, pulling her into my arms. I need to be surrounded by my woman for the whole night—to have her light shine through the ugly darkness of the last few days. I need her goodness to obscure the evilness of this world and guide me back to her always.

"Thank you, that was beautiful," she hums, filling my

heart with pleasure, knowing that my woman enjoyed what we just shared as much as me.

"You make it beautiful," I tell her as I close my eyes, content and at peace, even if it's just for the night. Having Freya in my arms safe is the only thing that relaxes me. When I phoned earlier and realized that she wasn't at the club but out and about, my fear that one of the Desperados would find her had my fear of losing her rising, overwhelming every thought in my mind.

When I saw her sitting, having coffee without a thought to her safety, I could have lost my shit, but the minute I saw her face all fear and worry disappeared. This woman in my arms calms my soul, my very mind. I will fight heaven and hell for her, she has become my very existence. I smile as I close my eyes in peace, hearing her breathing deepen in sleep.

FREYA 18

"Is he upset?" I can feel my stomach tense in nervousness when I think of what Tor will say. I feel like a schoolgirl again called to her teacher's classroom after school for something I did wrong.

Dane shrugs as he guides me towards Tor's office.

"Dane?" I call, irritated that he's not answering.

"What did you expect when breaking into his drawers?" he asks in a matter-of-fact voice.

I stop a couple of feet away from the office. "What will he do?"

"It will be fine, Freya, but he wants to talk to you and Anastasia." The knots in my stomach have grown and are now making me feel sick. I asked Dane if Tor was upset with him because we didn't listen, but he merely shrugged and now Tor wants to speak to us. Dane's finger is stroking my hand as he opens the door to Tor's office. The first person I see is Ulrich squatting down before Anastasia as she sits on the chair in front of Tor's desk. Walking in, I realize Tor isn't here.

"Looks like we're in trouble," Anastasia says as she glances at me.

"Where's Tor?" I ask as I sit down on the chair next to Anastasia.

"He's coming," Ulrich says as he stands, his muscles rippling as he throws a weary glance at Dane just as the door opens and Tor walks in. The first thing I notice is his scowl, he doesn't seem happy, and an unhappy Tor is not good for anyone. He walks around his desk and sits, facing us. At first, he doesn't say anything as he takes both of us in. I can feel my hands shaking slightly in nervousness until Dane's hand rests on my shoulder, which, in a tiny way, gives me comfort knowing that Dane won't let anything happen.

"Here at the club, we need to be able to trust everyone here…" Tor begins, his voice low as if talking to children. "Do the two of you think we can trust you when you break into things that are locked for a reason?"

"We just wanted to go out, Tor, you need to understand that we were locked at the club for two whole weeks," Anastasia argues, which has Tor leaning forward as he places his elbows on his desk.

"This is far from being a prison, Anastasia," he reminds her in a hard voice, "and if you felt so closed in, why didn't you ask your mate to take you out?"

I see Anastasia glance up at Ulrich. "To be fair . . ." Ulrich starts, but Tor lifts his hand to stop him.

"You had your turn earlier." That tells me that Tor has gone through this with the men before he called us in.

"Look, unfortunately it isn't always safe when you're with an Elemental, therefore, we have to make decisions to keep those around us safe. If you don't listen, then you're not safe, which will in turn, jeopardize my men's lives, and I don't like that."

"We didn't think," I murmur, understanding where he is coming from. I know that by Dane and Ulrich coming after us, we jeopardized the other men that they were with at the time.

"I need everyone in this club to pull together so we can keep you and everyone else safe." He looks at the men, his eyes a freezing blue. I sense that there is a message in his eyes that I don't know, but I feel that the men do. "I don't want this to happen again. If you want to go out gallivanting, then by all means, do it, but safely. I will make sure that the prospects are ready to accompany you when you want, but with one condition," his eyes bore into the two of us before he continues, "that your mates know what you are planning at all times."

I'm surprised he is consenting to having prospects accompany us whenever we need it. "Thank you," I say.

Anastasia nods her thanks.

"You can go," he says with a grunt which has me quickly standing to leave, just as we get to the door his words stop us again. "And next time you think to break into something that I've locked away, don't." His words are hard, forceful, and I know that out of everything, he is not pleased that we went into his locked drawer.

"Well, that wasn't very pleasant, now was it?" Anastasia mumbles.

"If you didn't decide to go and eat cake when I asked you not to go out, then you wouldn't have to listen to him," Ulrich argues as they make their way down the corridor.

"Which of you broke into his drawer?" Dane asks.

Looking up at him as we walk into the kitchen, I shrug. "Doesn't matter, does it?"

"I thought so," he says.

"What?"

"I knew it wasn't you."

"How did you know that?"

"Well, besides the fact that Tor has a camera in his office, I didn't feel that you were the one that went to get the key."

I'm afraid that I have to burst his bubble. "Actually, it was my idea to go out that gate." He places his arm around my shoulders, pulling me against him as we walk past the kitchen and towards the workshop. "Where are we going?"

"I know that the two of you wanted to do more than you did yesterday, so we all decided to go for a ride today as we need a time out."

I stop. "What about Esmeralda? Don't you need to find her or try to figure out everything in the book?"

"Tor and Asgar are staying behind to continue looking through the book. We are waiting for info from Celmund in regard to the coordinates, and if there is any connection with anything that we have suspected before or anyone that might work in the building."

"Does that mean that we will spend the whole day together?" We have had hardly any days alone together, so the fact that I will be with Dane the whole day has just improved my mood considerably.

"Hopefully, unless something happens," he says as he

lowers his head to kiss my lips.

"Come on, we are all waiting here," Colborn says loudly when Dane lifts his head. Looking over at them, I smile when I see the men on the bikes. Ulrich and Anastasia are just getting onto his Harley. Since being here at the club, I've learned to look at life differently. These men have shown me how protective and caring they can be, even if they're not family.

I've seen everyone pull together. Now that we are at war, I've noticed how worried they all are about each other. Looking at all of them you would never say how close they all are by the way they argue, or how different each one is, but when living with them, we see how they go out of their way for each other, something that I didn't see in the life I was living.

Tom phoned me again, to tell me that they had got someone else for the role in the movie and what a bad decision it was not taking it. I know that he's not happy because he lost out on a big commission with me not taking that role, but I still think it was the best decision I made by not taking it. I'm so much happier now; I feel like I can finally be myself.

I haven't heard anything from my mother. If she continues with her plan and tries to fight me in court for my money, saying that I'm not fit to make my own decisions, I might have to find a good lawyer as I don't want this out in the public domain for everyone to know. I still can't believe that she would do something like she did, or say something like that to me. I mean, we don't talk much, but I've always taken care of her even though she has never been a good mother.

The day she came here was the day that I decided that I needed to think about myself and see what made me happy. This relationship with my mother is toxic to me. I won't stop sending her money every month if she doesn't decide to take me to court, but if she does, then I will stop the monthly instalments I deposit in her bank account and forget that she's my flesh and blood. I let Dane guide me to the Harley, taking my helmet from him and placing it over my head.

"Are you ready?" Dane asks when we are both sitting on the bike, the others already pulling away.

"I'm ready."

I'm more ready than he knows. Now that I've decided to retire from being an actress, I need to do something else with my life, I know that as things are now, it will be difficult to do anything, but with time, I plan to start my own nursery. Planting and working with soil have always brought me peace and made me happy. I know that Dane might not like the idea of me being out every day, but it's better than me being away in some other country filming.

I have money to start the nursery, and make it successful, I will just need to get someone to help me with the office work as I hate paperwork. Looking at Ulrich and Anastasia that are riding next to me, I consider asking Anastasia to help me.

I know that Anastasia worked for a shipping company before meeting Ulrich. Now, besides trying to find ships that might be suspicious for the Elementals to investigate, and see if any women are being trafficked in them, she doesn't have anything that keeps her busy, and has complained to me more than once that she needs to find something to keep her occupied.

Anastasia and I have become friends. In all the time that we have been together, she has shown me that she is true to what she says, and that she is a true friend. I've never had a true friend like I have in Anastasia, and I'm pleased to know that she thinks the same about me.

When Dane turns, I frown when I see that we are riding into the city. I thought that we were just going for a ride, but it seems like we are going into the centre where Dane and Ulrich found us yesterday. A few minutes later we are all pulling up outside the little coffee shop where we met Esmeralda.

Again, looking inside, I see that the place is full. If everyone thinks of sitting inside, it will be a tight fit, as I don't think they have enough empty tables to accommodate everyone. Dane helps me off the bike, guiding me inside.

"They don't have enough sitting space," I murmur, only

to feel Dane squeeze my waist gently.

"Dag, Tal, and Einar are joining us later." Glancing over my shoulder, I realize that he's right and that the three men have crossed the road and are walking in different directions.

"Are they looking for Esmeralda?" I ask.

"From what you said, it sounds like she knows the coffee shop quite well, which means that she must be staying close by to walk here." Now that he says that, I remember something I saw on top of the table that I only remembered now.

"I forgot to tell you," I say as Dane sits on the chair next to me, "Esmeralda had a pamphlet on the table that she took with her of a laundromat," his back is to the wall as he faces the main door. Colborn sits on my right, then Anastasia with Ulrich next to her. Garth, Haldor and Eirik are sitting before us with their backs towards the door. It is clear that the staff aren't too thrilled to have so many dangerous looking bikers in a family bakery like this.

"Do you remember the name?" Eirik asks, but I shake my head in denial as I can't think of what the name was.

A little girl of about three comes to stand next to Haldor.

I smile when I see him tense. It is clear that he is

uncomfortable with the attention he is getting from her. The mother starts to call her, but the little girl is so fascinated with him that she doesn't pay her mother any attention. I signal the mom telling her it's okay, I can see the uncertainty on her face, but she stops calling her. The little girl lifts her hand and places it on Haldor's hand. "Pitty." At her touch, I swear he pales.

"She doesn't bite," I inform him.

"Yes, she does, look, she has teeth," he says softly as if telling me a secret.

I grin. "Well, she thinks you're pretty."

At my statement, his eyes widen, and I swear his face darkens with colour.

Garth grins at his embarrassment. "Damn, Haldor, looks like you have made another conquest."

Haldor grunts.

"Up," the little girl says as she lifts her hands to him. I see him glance over his shoulder at the mom, then back down at the little girl.

"Go to your mom," he whispers.

The little girl grins. "Up, up," she says again.

"Come on, Brother, pick the poor kid up and take her to her mom," Colborn says as he leans back, crossing his arms over his chest as he looks at the mom and winks.

"Don't flirt with the mom, you lug." Anastasia says.

"You take her," Haldor says in desperation. Is it possible that he has never picked a child up before?

"Haldor, just place your arms under her arms and pick her up."

He looks at me as if I've just grown a double head. "That's a bad idea," he grunts just as the girl decides that she has had enough of waiting and is now trying to climb up onto his lap by herself.

"Don't be an ass; pick the kid up," Dane says with a grin, knowing how uncomfortable Haldor is feeling.

"Fu. . ." he starts to say before snapping his mouth closed and looks down at the girl. "Okay, but stop moving." At his statement, I burst out laughing. Telling a kid to stop moving is like telling the sun to stop rising. He places his big hands under her tiny arms, circling her whole upper body as he picks her up off the floor, holding her out so he can look at her smiling face.

"What now?" he asks, looking to us for guidance.

The little girl starts kicking her legs in merriment as she laughs. "Pitty," she squeals, which has Haldor looking horrified. He stands, still holding the poor child away from his body as he makes his way towards her mother. As soon as he reaches the woman, he is placing the happy little girl in her arms. "Pitty," the little girl calls as he turns, making his way back to us.

"Hey, Pretty, have you decided what you want?" Garth teases, which has Haldor showing him the finger, making all of us laugh.

"You're a real heartbreaker, look at the poor kid," Anastasia says, "She's crying... she wants her pretty."

I see Haldor's face fall as he glances back to see the little girl looking at him with big sad eyes.

"Fuck," he scowls as he stands. "I'm going out to look for Dag's woman."

"No, don't go," I say, feeling bad that he's feeling uncomfortable and wants to leave. "She will quiet. Kids are like that. They cry when they can't get what they want."

He shrugs, making his way out the door, anyway.

"He is really uncomfortable around kids, isn't he?" I remark, watching him leave.

"It's not as if any of us have much to do with children," Colborn says just as the waiter comes over to our table.

"What can I get you?" *Well he's not very friendly, now is he?* The man's whole demeanour is unfriendly, which makes me uncomfortable.

Anastasia orders and then Dane orders for me and him, the rest of the men make their orders, asking for extra cups, which I'm guessing is for the others that are going to join us later, or maybe to take with them. I'm about to say something when I see Esmeralda on the other side of the road getting into a taxi.

"Look, it's her," I say just as she closes the door behind her. Everyone turns to look out the window.

"Her who?" Ulrich asks.

"It was Esmeralda, she just got into that taxi." One minute the men are sitting, the next Colborn, Garth and Eirik are off their chairs and hurrying out the door. Dane and Ulrich sit back looking out of the window at the other men that are starting up their Harleys.

"Dag," I glance to see Dane on his phone. "Colborn, Garth, and Eirik are after a taxi, which we saw your woman get into."

I hear Dag say something before the call is disconnected. "Do you think they will get to her?" I ask.

Dane nods as he lowers his head to kiss my forehead. "Good thing you were here, we might not have seen her," he says just as the waiter places all the food on the table.

"Are your friends coming back or should I prepare takeaways?" the waiter asks.

"No, it's fine, you can leave it," Ulrich says, waiting for the waiter to leave before he says, "more for us," which has Anastasia slapping his stomach playfully.

"You're such a glutton."

"Me? Nah," he says with a grin.

"I'm having Eirik's," Dane says, pulling Eirik's sandwich towards himself.

"Are you eating yours and his?" I ask with a frown.

"Well, I can't let it go to waste, now can I?" His double burger is already huge, but with Eirik's steak sandwich, I don't know how he can manage all the food. I smile shaking my head at his happy smile, one thing about the Elemental men is that they love their food, it's a good thing that they have a fast metabolism, or they wouldn't look as handsome on their Harley's as they do now.

I know that today is all about giving Anastasia and me a day out, but I'm glad that we have managed to see Esmeralda and maybe the men will be able to find her and keep her safe before she is caught. We finish eating without any sign from the others. Dane stands to go and pay, and I start making my way outside, smiling as I hear Anastasia and Ulrich bantering.

Opening the door, I step outside. The spring air surrounds me with its gentle breeze. I look back to see that the others are inside by the counter, laughing at something. Dane is grinning, his rugged features so handsome that I know there will never be a man more handsome to me. Hearing the squeal of tires, I'm still smiling when a van stops, the back-sliding door opens, and a man who jumps out suddenly starts running towards me. In that instant, I realize that I shouldn't have come outside alone.

"Dane," I scream but it's too late, as the man drags me towards the open door of the van. The last thing I see is Dane's eyes snap around to face me, his expression changing as he realizes what is happening, and then the sliding door of the van closing just as I see Dane rushing towards the Coffee shop's door.

DANE 19

My heart stops when I see the motherfucker pulling Freya into the van. "Motherfucker!" I roar as I charge outside, but the van is already pulling away. I could run after the van, but people would find it strange to see a human keeping up and maybe catching the moving van, so I jump on my bike, twisting the throttle as I ride after them. There is nowhere they can hide because I will follow them to the pits of hell to get Freya back.

I can hear Ulrich swearing as he follows, but I'm not waiting for him and Anastasia to catch up. These fuckers better not hurt Freya because I will skin them. My heart is racing, the image of Freya being pulled into the van keeps repeating in my head. I'm always supposed to keep my mate safe, but those sons of bitches took her from right under my eyes.

My anger is racing, for each second that passes with Freya in their hands, my control slips. They are speeding out of the city, thinking that they will lose me, but they have no idea that away from prying eyes, I will be able to unleash mayhem on them for touching what is mine. I'm just behind them when one of them starts shooting. Now that we are away from the main hustle and bustle, they think that they can dispose of me.

Lifting one hand off the handlebars, I bend the air. It is time to teach them that they should never mess with an Elemental. It's a shame that they won't survive to tell their boss that he messed with the wrong woman.

I make sure that the air is thick enough before casting it forward to encounter and block the van from its forward movement. The air will be so thick that they will find it difficult to drive forward. Freya could have stopped all of this when they first took her, but I saw the asshole covering her mouth when she called my name. That asshole had his dirty hands on her, hands that he will lose for touching her.

The van skids, the wheels spinning, but nothing happens as the van comes to a standstill. I bring my bike to a skidding stop. Jumping off before it has come to a complete stop, I run towards the van. Someone shoots at me again, but the air is still oppressing the forward movement so instead of the bullets coming for me they are falling uselessly to the ground.

Reaching the van, I yank at the sliding door with such anger that the whole panel comes away in my hands. I hear Ulrich coming to a stop, his bike idling as he assesses the situation. He knows that he can hang back as I can easily dispose these sons of bitches that thought they could take my woman. When the door is thrown to the ground, I see Freya lying on the floor of the van, her eyes closed in unconsciousness. The man standing over her is staring at me with a surprised expression, his hand is raised in supplication but there will be no forgiveness for him. The other two men in the front are still trying to understand why their guns aren't performing the way they would like them to.

Leaning in, I pull the asshole that thought he could touch Freya out and over my shoulder. He groans as he hits the verge of the road. My anger blinds me to everything except Freya. Touching her face, her eyes open, a dazed look in her eyes which tells me that she will be fine. There is a handprint on her cheek, which has me roaring in fury. I feel a presence a minute before I see a blade from the corner of my eye. Snapping my right hand towards it, I knock the blade out of the driver's hand, then with the same hand I grab his neck pulling him over the back of the seat towards me.

"What do you think you are doing?" my voice is low and full of rage. When they mess with an Elemental's mate, they should be prepared for death. His other hand rises and punches me in the face, the blow not phasing me with the amount of fury I have coursing through my body. Slipping my other arm around his neck, I pull him the rest of the way out of the van before tightening my grip until I hear him gasping, but even then I don't release my hold. If I had not been with Freya, they would have taken her, hurting her before I could even get to her.

When the bastard goes lax in my arms, I drop him to the ground. I hear running footsteps and know that the other man is running. He doesn't know this yet, but he will soon find out. He can run, but he won't be able to hide because I know who he is, and he will pay for being part of this kidnap attempt of my mate. I turn towards the man on the ground, stalking towards him I lean down picking him up by his neck with one hand.

"You touched my woman."

"Fu. . .fuck off." Pulling back my hand, I punch him across the face just where I saw Freya's marks. His head snaps back with the force, his nose immediately bleeding, but I don't stop as I shake him.

"You were saying?" I ask, the only thought coursing through my mind is that he hurt Freya. I let go of his neck, which has him slumping to the ground. I'm about to lean down to pick him up by his jacket to shake him when Freya interrupts me.

"Dane," her voice is low, urging my eyes to turn to look at her. She's sitting with her legs hanging out of where the sliding door was. Her expression tenses as she looks at me. "Stop..."

"He hurt you." I know she won't understand, but there is no way that I can let them get away with what they did, especially this fucker on the floor because he's the one that slapped her.

"I just want to go home," she whispers, but I can hear her. My woman's wishes will always come first. I know that she is trying to stop me from killing this fucker, but his fate was sealed the minute he touched her. I will concede and take her home letting her think that she has saved this asshole's life, but the truth is that I can hear bikes approaching which means that the others are close. They will take him, find the one that ran away, and dispose of the dead one.

Maybe not today, or even tomorrow, but soon I will have my time with them, and I will make them pay. Turning my back on the asshole, I step towards Freya; I would lose all sense of direction without her. It is the first time that she has referred to the club as home. The fact that she has accepted this new life so easily is all I could hope for. Freya is everything I want—everything I will ever want. "Let's go home." I slide my arm under her legs, picking her up against my heart. Her arms slide around my neck as she lays her head against my chest.

"I can walk," she reminds me.

"I know, but I would rather carry you." I make my way towards my bike, noticing that one of my men must have picked it up from where it fell on its side after I jumped off it to hurry towards Freya and her assailants.

"Is Freya okay?" Anastasia asks as she hurries towards us. Freya lifts her head from my shoulder to look over at Anastasia.

"I'm okay."

I see Garth and Tal making their way towards where the fucker is trying to crawl away. There is no escape for him, but I guess hope is the last thing you feel before you die. I sit Freya on my bike, making sure that it's not too damaged to ride back. There are a couple of scratches on the tank and the handlebar is slightly bent, but otherwise it's looking fine. Starting the Harley I turn to make my way back to the club. I see Garth has found the other asshole that ran off because as I open the throttle to make my way home, I see him carrying him to the van.

We are at war. Every attack on us will be dealt with. We will not leave ourselves open to defeat. We need to show them, and every other gang or MC that might want to come against us, that we are not weak.

"I'm sorry…"

Hearing Freya's apology I frown. Why the fuck would she be sorry? Placing one of my hands over her arms that are holding onto my waist, I squeeze gently.

"For what?"

"If it wasn't for Anastasia and me wanting to go out yesterday, we wouldn't have been at the coffee shop today and no one would have got hurt."

The fact that she is blaming herself for the attack has my anger rising again. "What happened wasn't your fault. Those assholes knew what they were getting into when they attacked." I want to stop the bike to look at her and make sure that she believes what I'm telling her, but I don't want to stop again. I look into the mirror, trying desperately to see her sad face behind me. I don't continue the conversation until we are back at the club and in our room.

"Look at me."

Freya is getting ready to shower, but before that, I want to make sure that she doesn't carry any unnecessary guilt with her.

Her eyes rise to meet mine with a question in them.

"I don't want you to feel guilty about what happened. We are at war and in every war, there are casualties. They knew what to expect if they tried to mess with one of our old ladies, and they purposefully continued."

"But if we hadn't gone out, that wouldn't have happened," she says shaking her head

"Sooner or later, we were going to go out. You wouldn't have been at the club eternally, and knowing them, they would have tried something like this then." Approaching her, I place my hands around the back of her neck, my thumbs raising her chin so that she's looking at me.

"I don't like violence, Dane," she murmurs.

"I know you don't, but in my life, violence sometimes is necessary. Freya, I need you to trust me. Trust me to do only what I think is right, and to keep you and the others safe."

I feel her muscles tensing at my statement, her eyes tormented. "I worry that you will get arrested one of these days for all the violence. How am I going to help you out of something like that?"

I lower my head to kiss her lips gently. My woman is worried about me. "Don't worry about me, Freya, I will not be arrested. I've lived for three hundred and twenty years, and in all that time I've never been arrested. I appreciate that you are worried, but, baby girl, there is no need."

She raises her hands to my chest. "Promise?"

I smile. "Have I told you yet that I love you?"

Her eyes widen. "Oh, that is so sneaky," she says. "You say that now so I will forget what we are talking about. I see your colours, Dane."

"What do my colours say?" I ask in amusement.

"The colours say that I love you, too." I feel my stomach tighten when I hear the words that I've been waiting to hear since the moment I bonded with my woman. I know that it's unnecessary for her to tell me that she loves me because as a bonded Elemental, we exist for each other. I want to be able to know my woman wants me in every way—not just because of our unbroken bond, but because she realizes, like I do, that there is nothing else out there that can compare to what we feel for each other.

I know that being my old lady will be a feat, not only because of our differences, but because of my quick temper and rash decisions. But one thing I'm certain of is that Freya will do anything in her power to save me from myself, even though I don't need saving. To know that you have someone in your life that is willing to give everything for you, fills my heart, letting me finally feel an all-consuming peace with life—a peace that I didn't feel before, and that only my woman can ever give me.

Elementals may be my roots, and the club my drive, but Freya is my very life—a life that can only be complete with her in it.

THE END.

A MESSAGE FROM ALEXI FERREIRA

Thank you so much for reading DANE and FREYA's book. This is book two in the Elemental's CT MC series. I hope you enjoyed your journey into the life of these bad boy alpha bikers and their women. **If you enjoyed this book, please consider leaving a review. Reviews help authors like me stay visible and help bring others to my series**. Next book in the Elemental's will be DAG.

DAG (Elementals CT MC) book 3

ESMERALDA 1

I can sense danger approaching, I am so tired of running, why can't they just give up? It has been months now and still The Desperados are after me. I thought that after slipping Sean's notes into one of the Elemental's Cape Town MC old ladies' bags that they would resolve the issue with The Desperados and they would stop coming after me, but no such luck. To be fair, they did do something, because Sean has disappeared from the picture and Basil has stepped up as the leader for The Desperados street gang.

Picking up my meagre belongings I prepare to slip away once again, I know that stealing Sean's ledger was stupid, but I had to try and stop them, stop him. I was sold to Sean when I was but seventeen to pay off a debt, luckily for me, or unluckily I'm still trying to decide which. Sean took a liking to me and decided that he wanted to keep me instead of selling me off like they do with so many other women.

It is going onto six years now, and only a few months ago did I manage to get away. I know that if they find me I will be dead, I know that stealing from The

Desperados is something they don't take lightly, but I had to try and do something. I have tried to get out of Cape Town, but everywhere I turn I see one of the men.

I know that I am fighting a losing battle and that sooner or later I am going to be found and then I will be made to pay for my crime. I might not have stopped the trafficking or the abuse, but at least I managed to get rid of Sean. At night when I fall asleep, I still dream that he is out there, always watching. My hand creeps up to scratch the scars at my wrist. It was a dark time in my life, a time that death would have been preferable to what I was going through, but Sean never let me slip away. Now he has gone, but still, I'm on the run.

Opening the door to the little bedroom that I managed to rent under false pretence, I quickly slip out, closing the door quietly behind me I keep to the shadows as I make my way towards the hole in the fence that I found a few weeks earlier. I slip through the hole and then I am mingling with the people walking up the street towards the waterfront.

The hoodie that I am using covers most of my hair and body, it hasn't been easy these months that I have been in hiding. I have exhausted every venue I could think of, initially I worked for a few weeks in a kitchen, but once the owner found out that The Desperados were looking for me, he apologized but he didn't want to get mixed up with gangs, therefore he would need to let me go.

Next, I managed to find a part-time at a laundromat but one night when I was leaving one of the gang members saw me and pursued, but luckily I managed to give him the slip, but again I couldn't go back to work. It has been like that since I ran, and to make matters worse the Elementals are also looking for me.

Sometimes I think that I should just give myself up, but to who? In my eyes one will kill me, and the others will exploit my knowledge and who knows what else until I again wish for a speedy death. I hear running footsteps in the distance and know that it is time to hurry up because those footsteps I know.

Sean found out about my gift a couple of months after being sold to him, he used to call me his secret weapon. He made sure no one found out about me and tried to keep me away from everyone as much as possible. I have a rare ability that I can enhance my senses to hear, see, smell and sense things so much more than the normal human. That is what has been saving me from everyone that has been trying to capture me. Slipping into an alleyway I hurry to an abandon building which I found a couple of weeks ago. I know that its just as dangerous in there as it is out here, but at least I can try to keep safe from the elements, besides, I don't think that they would suspect that I was hiding right under their very noses.

I can hear movement inside but know that it's the two homeless men that live there, finding the broken window I slip inside trying to be as quiet as possible as I would rather, they also not know that I am here, because if they can sell my whereabouts, I am sure they will.

Opening the door to the little closet that I spied out the other day, I slip inside. I will be as warm and as safe as possible in here. It doesn't smell all that great but the same way that I can enhance my senses, luckily, I can also close them off. Pulling my hoodie off I place it on the ground so that I can sit on it. There must be something more to life then this constant turmoil.

Since I can remember that I have been pushed from one place to another. My mother was a drug addict, doing anything for her next fix, when she died, I was handed to my grandmother that didn't miss a chance to remind me every opportunity that she got of what a useless burden I was on her, that is until she used me to pay the debt she had with The Desperados.

Sean was a mean bastard that would do anything for a buck, when he found out about my gift, he made sure that I used it at every opportunity to help him acquire his fortune. A tear slips down my cheek, no matter how much time passes, the pain of what I did for him never becomes easier. I was his way in with the women that they kidnapped, I would strike up a conversation and then bring them to him.

He would have me find them like a blood hound,

sniffing them out so he could make money. I don't know what it is about the women he had me find, but all of them had a particular fragrance to them and funny enough the two women that I met at the coffee shop a couple of months ago that belong to the Elementals CT MC had the same fragrance, I slipped Sean's ledger into their bag hoping that they would give it to the Elementals which would hopefully find a way to stop him.

Initially I would fight Sean, but with time I found it easier to submit then to fight as the scars on my body will profess. I was his plaything, his personal rabbits' foot, as he would say, but in the end I was also his destruction. I was hoping to stop the whole sickening business they had going, but I need to be happy with the Elementals having defeated Sean.

When the Elementals woman told me that they had gone to war with The Desperados because of me, not that they knew it was me as I didn't tell them my name, I was surprised. Why would a group of men go to war because of a woman that they didn't even know, but then I realized that they must have been looking for the information that I stole.

I figured that if they could find it useful and maybe stop what was happening, then I would give them the ledger. Unfortunately, I think that they are thinking that I have more information because they are still looking for me. It is already difficult to hide from one crime organization like The Desperados that are one of Cape Town's most feared gangs, but now I have the most notorious motorcycle club looking for me too.

There is something different about them though, as their tread seems to be softer but more assured. I can tell when they are close by the softer sounds they make, but also by the static energy that starts to approach. There is one energy in particular that perturbs me, it calls me in instead of drawing me away. I have been curious to find out who's energy it belongs to, but I am scared that they will find me if I get too close and I must be honest they have come closer than anyone ever should and somehow, they keep on finding me. I still don't know how they do it, but they find me in the most unexpected places.

Closing my eyes, I sigh, the one thing that I would really like is to have a full night of uninterrupted sleep. I would like a night where I felt safe and that no one was going to find me, a night of peace but even if I fall asleep my dreams wake me up. I clutch the backpack close to my chest, the meagre belongings that I have are in the backpack, I don't have anything of value as I was never able to acquire anything worth keeping throughout my life and everything I had while with Sean was given to me.

When younger I had very little, my mother didn't have the money for anything except drugs, and when I went to my gran, she only acquired the essentials needed for me not to embarrass her. Placing the haversack on the ground I lay down with my head on it, my body is curled into a ball to try and maintain my body heat, but the cold of the floor is starting to seep through the hoodie into my very bones. I have no one to turn to, my father I never knew who it was, and throughout my life I was never able to make friends.

I dream of one day having a life where I can be at peace, the only thing I want out of life is to be at peace. Most people are usually after riches to be happy, or romance. Me, I'm only looking for peace and no matter how much I think about it, I can't find a road that leads me to that peace. It has been my dream throughout my life, I remember when I was young hearing a woman say to another that some people are born under a lucky star and others are just unlucky. Unfortunately for me, I think I am one of those that was born under an unlucky star.

I tense when I hear the rats scurrying about, but because there is nothing in here, I am hoping that they will stay away. One of the men grunts as he moves about, but after a while, he quietens. My senses tell me that for now I am safe, but for how long? things tend to change quickly, and I need to be prepared.

This is the safest place at the moment in the building as it keeps me away from the men that squat here, and it keeps me marginally warm for the night, but tomorrow I need to find a better place to hide, a place that has an escape route that is easily accessible as this tiny little room is closed in and no where to hide or run.

I am only twenty-three, but I believe that I have an old soul, a tired soul. Sometimes I wonder why I was born into this life, a life that has brought me nothing but pain. My hair falls over my face obscuring the pitch darkness where I find myself. Luckily, I had a chance to shower today before sensing that they were closing in on me. My long black hair is clean, I have been tempted to cut it since I started running but I believe that it's my only good feature. My dark green eyes are too large for my face, my lips are too pouty, and my skin isn't the light peachy colour that makes woman so beautiful, instead I have a dark honey tone that luckily hides certain scars, I guess for the life that I have had it's the best type of skin, a lily-white tone would show all the bruises that I have had throughout the years.

I suddenly tense, there is a light rustle different from the other sounds. I wait to try and hear it again, but it doesn't repeat itself, if anyone catches me in here I am done for. I have nothing to protect myself, not even a bat and there is no where I can hide. I don't know how long I lie stiffly listening to the sounds outside, I hear a couple talking somewhere down the street, their playful words have a sad smile lifting my lips.

I hope their happiness lasts for a very long time, I have become tinted to love, have never felt love for anyone. I loved an old dog that used to hang around near where my gran lived, and every chance I got I used to creep out and feed him, but one day he just stopped appearing. I took food out for him for weeks after his disappearance, but he never came back. Since then, I learned never to hold onto anything, because sooner or later it leaves.

There banter starts to lull me to sleep, my body cold but too tired to care. I must have dozed because the next thing I know I am snapping awake from a dream, the same dream where Sean is still alive, and he has found me. He is torturing me for having disobeyed, torturing me worse than he ever has before. My breathing is loud in my ears, my cheeks wet from the tears. Sean was evil, evil to his very rotten core.

Sitting up I listen; I must have been asleep for a while because the sounds outside are minimal which tells me that it must be the middle of the night or very early morning. Stretching out my legs I pull the haversack towards me to open the outside pouch. Pulling out the little bag of dried meat I take a strip and slowly start to chew. In the olden days people used to live off dried strips of meat and water, for now I still have a few strips which I need to make sure lasts me for a while until I can find another job and place to live, or until I finally find my way out of Cape Town.

Today I will once again try to approach the train station and see if the men are still there on the lookout, I know that they are at the bus stop because I checked yesterday. I can't make it on foot out of Cape Town because I'm scared that they will find me hitchhiking and bring me back. I tried to hide in a truck that was going to Johannesburg once, but the driver found me and kicked me out.

I hear footsteps, these are quite a distance away, but I recognize them as belonging to the Elementals. What is this Elemental doing by himself at this time of night walking the streets of Cape Town. His steps are unhurried as he walks. I open up my senses and immediately sigh when I feel the energy of this particular Elemental, it is the one that calls to me, the one that calms me, but today I sense something else. Closing my eyes, I focus only on his energy, today there is a feeling of sadness radiating from him. I don't know this man, but my heart tightens in sorrow for him.

"What's wrong?" I whisper, I have an overwhelming feeling of hugging him close until his sadness dissipates. His footsteps have stopped, I wonder what he's doing?

"Esmeralda?" I tense when I hear my name on his lips, it's not possible, did he hear my whisper? No, I'm sure it's coincidence because the only person that could hear that whisper is me. Is he looking for me? Why would he be out at this time of night still looking for me?

"Can you hear me?" once again I whisper, but as soon as I say the words, I shake my head smiling sadly. I think that I am so lonely that the thought of this man hearing me, pleases me. It's clear that it was a coincidence him saying my name just after I asked him what was wrong, but it made me feel like we were somehow connecting.

"Yes, I can hear you." What? how? My hand lifts to my mouth to keep the gasp in. That's not possible, I know that he's quite a distance away, that would mean that he has very keen hearing like me. I can feel my heart racing, I'm not sure if it's racing in fear or excitement that there is someone else out there that has the same disability as me. "Don't hide from me, I want to help you." His words are soft but clear, seeming closer. I wish I could believe him, wish that I could just throw caution to the wind and go out to meet him, but I know that I couldn't survive the tortures that I endured before with Sean.

I have seen the Elementals before and I know that they are not easy men, they are hard dangerous men. Men that take what they want, when they want it. I have nothing else to give, everything has been taken from me, the only thing left is my life, and I will be damned if I will give up my life without a fight.

It wasn't just the physical pain but the mental pain that Sean imposed on me, the constant torture eating away at my soul every day. I can't let that happen again; I can't let myself be caught by anyone. I have learnt throughout life that there is no happy life for me, that I need to make my own happiness in my own way.

"Esmeralda, talk to me." His hypnotic tones call to me, but I hold my hand firmly over my mouth, I would like nothing more than to have a conversation with him, but I won't because if he can hear me, maybe he can also sense me? If so, he can easily find me here if I continue our dialogue.

Maybe if I were somewhere where I knew it would be easy to escape if he was close, I would encourage this conversation, but in a little closet in a dilapidated building with no way to escape is not the time to do it.

"Esmeralda, let me help you." His words are sad, but there is an underlying note of truth to them "let me protect you." I wish I could believe him, could trust his word, but I can't.

TO BE CONTINUED IN DAG (ELEMENTALS CT MC) book 3

ABOUT THE AUTHOR

Alexi Ferreira, loves the idea of Alpha Men who take charge are possessive and care for their woman. She creates books that take you on an emotional journey whether tears, laughter or just steamy hotness. She loves to connect with readers and interacting with them through social media or even old fashioned email.

She currently lives in the United Kingdom. Books she has written are:

- Wulf (Book 1) Elemental's MC
- Bjarni (Book 2) Elemental's MC
- Brandr (Book 3) Elemental's MC
- Ceric (Book 4) Elemental's MC
- Bion (Book 5) Elemental's MC
- Cassius (Book 6) Elemental's MC
- Celmund (Book 7) Elemental's MC
- Burkhart (Book 8) Elemental's MC
- Caelius (Book 9) Elemental's MC
- Draco Salvation (Book 10) Elemental's MC
- Draco Wrath (Book 10) Elemental's MC

- Tormented (Book 1) Bratva Fury
- Turmoil (Book 2) Bratva Fury
- Mayhem (Book 3) Bratva Fury
- Fury (Book 4) Bratva Fury

Join her Social Media platforms to stay up to date as well as take part in giveaways and just let her know how you feel about her books!

Link: https://www.alexiferreira.writer.com/subscribe

WULF (Book 1) in the Elemental's MC series.

WULF

She is mine, they can try and get to her but they won't succeed, I will go through hell to protect her. No one touches what is mine. I will shake the earth itself, no one will be safe. My brothers and I are a family the club is my home but she is my soul the light to my darkness.

JAS

I have always felt like I didn't belong. Until I met Wulf. He takes me away from everything I know and introduces me to a life that I never expected. Now instead of being alone I have the whole mc as family, but I am in danger. Before everyone treated me as if I was a freak. But he understands me.

TORMENTED (book 1) Bratva Fury series.

JADE
I was minding my own business, simply working until Alexei the boss for the bratva mafia decided to take me. Having run away from a violent man before, I made a promise to myself this wouldn't happen again, but he doesn't give me a choice. I'm thrown into a world of violence, but this man of such vengeance almost hatred towards some can offer such love and safety when in his arms, something I have never experienced before.

ALEXEI
There's a war looming, hanging overhead like a dark cloud. This is the worst time to allow somebody into my life, but when I laid eyes on jade all logic and rational thought left me. I will protect her even if from herself, whoever comes for me is one thing, but to harm her will mean certain death, even if it kills me trying. She is my everything, my reason to live and if fate wants it, my reason to die.

BOUND (book 1) Wolverine MC.

HUNTER
I have wondered if I would ever find my soulmate, the woman that would calm my soul. Now that I've found her she is mine, she just doesn't know it yet. Her ex thinks that he can stalk my woman and there will be no repercussions , well he has terrorized her enough. I will make sure that no one ever hurts her again. Anyone that tries to mess with her will have to deal with me and the whole WOLVERINE MC.

DAKOTA
This is a bad idea, but when I'm with hunter I feel safe, and wanted, something that I haven't felt in a long time. He has my heart racing with a single glance, there is a bond between us that I can't deny. Being part of an mc is intimidating, but they are protective and like family, I know it's a mistake but I have never felt more at home or complete as I do now.

Printed in Great Britain
by Amazon